Penny Appleton

Love, Second
Time Around

A SUMMERFIELD VILLAGE
SWEET ROMANCE

Love, Second Time Around
Copyright © Penny Appleton (2017). All rights reserved.

www.PennyAppleton.com

ISBN: 978-1-912105-84-7

Requests to publish work from this book should be sent to:
penny@pennyappleton.com

Cover and Interior Design: JD Smith Design
Typeset in 16pt Minion Pro

CURL UP
PRESS

www.CurlUpPress.com

Chapter 1

It's dawn and raining hard on a Thursday in Summerfield, but my garden robin is an optimist. He pours his liquid song from the top of a birch tree, telling the world it's spring, even as leaves blow wildly across the lawn.

I smile and check that the back door and windows are locked as I walk through my cottage. A faint aroma of toast lingers in the warm kitchen, and my big Aga stove purrs quietly as it adjusts the central heating.

As I pass the breakfast bar, I touch the photos of my wonderful children hanging on the wall behind. Samantha, grinning at Luke on their wedding day, and Harry, surfing with friends. I pause to look more closely at the lovely one of the three of us laughing together, Mother's Day two years ago, with glasses of champagne in our hands. Happy days, indeed.

I check the dining area next to the kitchen, the center of so much of our family life. I remember Harry, aged nine, sitting at the old oak table, his legs curled around the chair, busy drawing monsters. I look up at the collection of antique milk jugs on the top shelf above, each a chipped and lovely treasure, discovered in Oxford flea markets with my daughter, Sam.

But there's no time for memories now. I check my watch again, switch off the light, and go into the sitting room.

Like many old English cottages, the front door opens into this living space opposite the narrow staircase, but I don't use it much. The back door is nearer to the garage and a much better place for storing coats and boots, muddy from walking the fields in the early mornings.

It's getting lighter outside and I cross to the window that looks out onto the driveway. It's still raining, and there's no sign of the taxi. It's not late, and there's plenty of time, but I'm eager to get going. I feel a pitter-patter of nerves and breathe, exhaling deeply. I know it will be okay, but this is the first conference since my retirement last year, and I want it to go well. As much as I love this cottage, it needs a lot of upkeep, so I need the work.

My familiar leather briefcase, raincoat, and overnight bag wait on a chair by the door. There is nothing left to do, so I straighten the cushions again and re-fold the throws on the two soft couches. The logs are stacked in the big, open fireplace and the kindling is laid, all ready for when I get home.

I love this room on wild winter nights, all curled up and cozy in the firelight. My Moroccan rug covers half the floor in a palette of reds and blues against a pattern of gray, polished flagstones. The low oak coffee table has two neat piles of books and the latest Horse Magazine that I'm looking forward to reading when I get back. I'm excited about this trip, but no matter how many times I leave, I always want to return to Square Cottage.

Headlights flash across the wall, and a white taxi turns through the gray dawn into the drive. I open the front door and wheel out my bag, eager to get going.

"Taxi to Oxford Station?"

"Morning, Jim." I smile as he climbs out of the driver's seat and touches his cap. He takes my overnight bag. "What's with the cap-touching formality?"

"Just practicing to be the Summerfield taxi driver of choice, Maggie."

"Good job, but you're the *only* Summerfield taxi

driver." I chuckle as I turn back to ruffle my fingers through a bowl of rose potpourri by the door. The scent of summer fills the air, and I know it will linger in the cottage until I get back. Grabbing my raincoat and briefcase, I pull the front door shut behind me, duck my head, and hurry through the rain to the taxi.

"Early start?" I brush water droplets off my suit as Jim reverses into the lane. My friend Selena waves from her bedroom window above The Potlatch Inn next door, and I wave back with a smile.

"You're the first today," Jim says, "but I had a terrible one yesterday. 3:00 a.m. to central London for the Eurostar."

I make sympathetic noises and turn to look back at Square Cottage as we drive away. It's three hundred years old with ashen stone walls and a darker gray roof rising to a central chimney on the top. It looks like a cottage teapot without a handle or a spout.

I fell in love with it when we first looked over the gate--Samantha, Harry and me, a little family in need of a home. The cottage was run down and broken. Patching it up took all my savings, but in rebuilding it, we became even closer, and together, we turned it into our family home. Those were happy years, and now that the children are grown up, I'm content living here on my own.

Most of the time.

Jim peers at the road ahead through the driving rain. "Excuse me for not talking, Maggie. The bends are slippery, and wet leaves are everywhere."

I nod and relax with the swish-swish of windshield wipers and faint music from the radio. From the back seat, I can just see my reflection in Jim's rearview mirror. My hair is shoulder length and still my natural corn-blonde color, with a bit of professional help. It's twisted into a smooth chignon today.

The executive businesswoman, professional but not distracting. Good enough. I comb the soft wisps around my face with my fingers and check to see that I'm wearing both earrings. A lesson learned from the past – hurrying out the door, juggling two kids and a demanding job.

I stare out at the rain-drenched fields passing by. Soon we're into Oxford and pulling onto the station forecourt, where Jim helps me with my bags.

"Have a good trip, Maggie."

A chilly wind blows across the station as Jim waves from the driver's window and pulls out into the early morning traffic. I pull my raincoat tighter around me. There's just enough time to buy a newspaper and a coffee before the train pulls in on Platform 7.

It's busy, but I find my reserved seat quickly, take off my coat, and settle into my seat. A shrill whistle echoes along the platform, and the train slides out of the station exactly on time. As we leave the suburbs of Oxford, I drink my coffee and look out at vivid green fields with cows and horses by the edge of the river. There are boats moored under the willow trees, their branches trailing in the current.

Rain slashes diagonally across the windows as the train gets up to speed. I read the news headlines, but I'm distracted. There's so much riding on this conference.

Just after Reading station, the train slows down.

After a few minutes at this reduced speed, it stops completely.

My heart beats faster, and I keep looking at my watch. The minutes tick by faster as the train finally begins to move again, but creeps along by inches.

I turn to the lady next to me. "Any idea why we're going so slowly? I didn't see anything on the train app."

"Something to do with the flooding. I did this journey earlier in the week, and we went at a snail's pace. Could be a while."

I try and stay calm, but I can't miss that flight.

Finally, we pull into Paddington. The doors unlock and I half-jog across the station, dragging my wheelie bag. I make it to the Heathrow Express to find a line of frustrated people and a Cancelled sign. I don't wait to see what the problem is, I just turn and puff my way to the station entrance, where black London taxis crawl in and out like ants. I join the funnel of commuters and finally make it to the front of the line.

The price to Heathrow makes me wince, but there's no alternative. My anxiety rises and rises as the taxi inches out of the city and onto the motorway toward the airport. My calm day has fallen apart. I'm disheveled now, my hair and makeup no longer perfect. The rain and wind and running around have flushed my cheeks, and my hair is flyaway. I do my best to touch it up in the back of the cab.

When we arrive at the airport, I thrust money at the driver and sprint to Check-in, making it just before it closes. Of course, there's a long security line, and I shift from foot to foot, trying to calm my breathing.

Come on, come on or I'm still going to miss the flight.

Cell phone and laptop out, liquids in their plastic bag. I take off my coat and suit jacket and slip them into the tray. Counting precious seconds, I silently plead with the security guy to ignore my shoes.

"Shoes off," he says.

"Final call for the remaining passenger on flight BA1434 to Edinburgh. Your flight is ready to depart, and all other passengers are waiting for you."

I run to the gate, blushing as I dash into the cabin. I'm the last to board, and the attendant closes the door behind me. I'm out of breath, flushed, and flustered.

So much for my careful planning and preparation.

I look down at my ticket. Window seat, 12A. Thank goodness it's quite near the front, so I don't have to walk the length of the cabin in embarrassment.

A man stands in the aisle, stowing his bag in the overhead locker. I wait to squeeze by and he turns as he closes it.

"Thank you."

I glance up. The man smiles down at me with dark, intelligent eyes behind stylish, black glasses. He's tall with close-cropped silver hair and a strong, close-shaven jawline. He wears a charcoal business suit expertly tailored to his athletic frame, and he smells of pine forests after rain.

My eyes widen. I take a breath, but suddenly, there's not enough air.

Greg Warren.

I freeze, my eyes locked on his face.

"Hello, Maggie," he says, in the beautiful American voice I haven't heard in so many years.

Chapter 2

"Please take your seats."

The flight attendant hovers anxiously. Greg slides into his row and I quickly walk by to take my seat further back, heart pounding.

So close, and yet there are so many years between us now.

I click my seatbelt as the plane moves onto the runway. Shock, then joy and wonder swirl through me, and I put a hand up to my hot cheeks. I thought he was gone from my heart.

I'm distracted and don't hear the safety talk through the tumble of memory. The plane accelerates, and with a subtle lift of the nose, we're climbing into the rain. A few minutes later, the seatbelt sign goes off, and Greg takes out his laptop. I stare out at the clouds, remembering the last time we met. The last time we said goodbye.

* * *

Los Angeles. Our final project review after a successful environmental campaign.

"You're not interested in moving Stateside, are you, Maggie?" the HR manager asked me, as we hugged goodbye. "There's a good job available with my new Division."

"Thanks for thinking of me." I shake my head. "But it's just not possible right now. Samantha and Harry need to stay in England, close to our family and friends."

"Maybe another time." She walked toward the door. "Take care and stay in touch."

It had been a successful project. We had managed to stop a factory complex from polluting a river and restored a natural wilderness area. I was so proud of the work we'd done, but the end had arrived. We had celebrated, and now it was time to go home.

The others had all gone, but my flight back to London was late, so I stayed in the hotel conference room typing up my notes.

The door opens. Greg walks in, his easy smile turning my head as it has done since the day we met three years ago. I don't want to say goodbye.

He walks over, and tears well in my eyes. I fight them back.

"Thanks for all your hard work, Maggie." His dark eyes are warm. Electricity flickers between us. "I've enjoyed working with you."

He shakes my hand and then pulls me in for a hug. We hold each other. The tears spill over, and I can't hold them back.

Greg's happily married. I've met Rachel, his wife, and seen pictures of his kids. Nothing has ever happened to say that he feels anything for me, and I made sure I was never alone with him, in case he guessed.

But in the three seconds too long that he holds me close, I know there's something between us.

As we pull away from each other, he takes a breath and sighs a little. "Safe journey."

He walks toward the door.

"Greg."

He halts but doesn't turn. The energy between us is on the verge of bursting into flame. If he turned now, I would be in his arms.

"Goodbye, Maggie," he whispers, and steps through the door, shutting it softly behind him.

I stand alone in an empty meeting room. If anyone looked in, they would see a blonde woman in a business suit, staring down at a computer screen. But behind the professional image, I'm overwhelmed with grief for the end of a love that never was.

* * *

Rain hammers the plane window as we head north to Scotland and I wonder how Greg Warren could possibly be back in my life.

When we land in Edinburgh, he stands, and our eyes meet. We smile, like acquaintances over a half-forgotten memory. He grabs his carry-on and walks off the plane with purpose. I stay in my seat, shaking my head at my inability to speak. I could have said something.

I should have.

But no, the past is best left in the past.

Then a thought enters my mind. What if he's going to the same conference?

A bubble of excitement expands inside me.

I meet Mike, the team leader for the environmental group, at baggage claim and we catch up on the agenda on the way into central Edinburgh.

At the hotel, we check in and head to the Balmoral Room. I find my name card on one side of the long conference table and am pleased to be near the door. I like to watch the faces around the table as well as the presentations on the screen at the opposite end.

"Coming to lunch?" Mike asks.

"I'll be down in a minute. I just need to get on Wi-Fi. Meet you down there."

Mike nods and leaves me in the room alone. I just need a minute to collect myself and, as I've been out of the game awhile, there's just something I want to check.

I type in the Wi-Fi password and connect my laptop quickly, then walk around the other side of the table for a quick scan of the name cards. I vaguely recognize a couple of them, and then I make it to the top of the table to the name card for the oil consortium team leader.

Back then, we worked together on the environmental cause, but now Greg Warren is the opposition.

The door opens, and Jude West, one of the government facilitators, comes through the door.

"Maggie!" He wraps me in a bear hug. "Glad you could come at short notice. Andrew McLean's got the flu."

"Tough for Andrew, but great for me. Lovely to see you, Jude. Are you busy?"

"Frantic with the escalating crisis in North Sea oil. The Department of the Environment needs a firm agreement on funding by year end, so we've got three important meetings in the next three months. Could you be here for all three? It would help with continuity."

"Yes, it's all good. I noted the dates from Mike's email, in case you asked."

I'm thrilled to hear about the potential for more work. I'll be able to get my roof fixed before winter, after all.

We talk about the details as we head to lunch, and although I'm prepared for Greg to be in the restaurant, my heart still skips a beat when I see him. People mill about holding plates and glasses, exchanging civil greetings before we enter official negotiations. Jude hands out name badges and introduces people. He ushers Greg over to me.

"Greg Warren, meet Maggie Stewart."

"We've met." Greg smiles and holds out his hand. I look into his eyes and smile back.

"It's been a long time, Greg. Good to see you." I manage to keep a professional tone, but his touch sends a tingling, electric current through me. I love the feel of his large hand wrapped firmly around mine. There's so much to say, but I have to keep my cool. He will be opposite me in that boardroom soon enough.

One of the oil delegation arrives and pulls Greg away. He looks back, a question in his eyes. I turn away, grab a salad from the buffet, and take it to a small table in the corner. Many of the delegates stand, walk about, and talk while eating, but I want to sit down. I need a moment to think, but I can also observe the power play in the room while I eat.

And there's a lot of politics going on here.

I watch Greg expertly work the room, a friendly touch here, a kind smile there. I can't help but remember the day he hired me. The year my marriage finally disintegrated. By the end of that bitter time, I was desperate to get away from Edinburgh, terrified at the thought of bringing up two kids on my own, and I needed to make more money.

With our home gone, we were staying with my Mum in Leith, just outside Edinburgh. There were tears and disturbed nights with the children, but I was determined to make a better life for them.

An interview came up in Banbury, near Oxford, at the British headquarters of an American oil company. I had worked in a law office since completing my degree and managed their contracts for the North Sea. They were expanding operations in Scotland and looking for someone to ensure that they complied with environmental legislation. It was several levels above my current work, and in a male-dominated field, but hey, what did I have to lose?

It was years ago now, but it seems like yesterday. We changed our lives that night, but we lost something too. I remember the night I told my Mum about the interview.

* * *

Samantha and Harry are asleep when I get back. I creep upstairs to kiss their sweet faces and tuck the covers tighter around them, and then I head down the narrow staircase to the kitchen. It's the only truly warm place in the house, a combination of the Scottish weather and Mum's tight budget.

"How did it go?" She sits at the kitchen table and pours out two china cups of tea. Mugs are too heavy for her wrists, so she uses the pink floral tea service she inherited from her Mum. Everything is the same as when my sister Jeannie and I grew up here before Dad died, even down to the oil cloth on the table.

Why would I throw it out, Maggie? It still has wear in it.

"I was pretty nervous." I rest my elbows on the table and warm my hands around the cup. "Three guys in suits, definitely out to give me a hard time. After two aggressive questions that were clearly intended to unnerve me, I hit them with some new data that opened their eyes a bit. Their company is by no means squeaky clean. They're open to litigation all over the place."

"You look so fierce when you're on the warpath, Maggie. Elbows off the table, dear."

"Aye." I sit back obediently, grinning at her as I exaggerate my accent. My soft Edinburgh burr turns into Dad's Highland growl. "But I know my stuff, Mum. I wasn't going to let them put me down. So I might have been a wee bit more feisty than usual."

She makes a tutting noise, but a smile plays around her lips.

"It turned out that they are having some real issues," I continue, sipping the hot tea. "I showed them how much they needed me. I was having fun by then and didn't see a man enter at the back of the room. Greg Warren, the new American General Manager." My eyes sparkle as I remember his words, and I feel proud of what I did today."He offered me the job, Mum."

"Congratulations, Maggie. Maybe we can have a wee dram to celebrate?"

Her words are heartfelt, but I know she's unhappy about us leaving Scotland. Mum has suffered a lot in her life, and she has developed a way of holding herself, pretending everything is okay. But the bright blue eyes in her lined face betray the agony she's feeling. I stand and go around the table, wrapping my arms around her hunched shoulders.

"I'm so sorry," I whisper, my cheek against her hair. "We'll come back lots, I promise, and you can come down on the train as often as you want."

* * *

The job on Greg's team meant a fresh start for the kids and me, but we lost having a Mum and Grandma nearby, and she lost all of us from her daily life. Dad was gone and Jeannie was off traveling, so after Mum died, I sold the house. It feels odd to be back in Edinburgh again, not three miles away from where everything changed.

Across the room, Frances Campbell, the current Environmental Officer for the oil consortium, leans up to whisper something in Greg's ear. He smiles at her, and I feel a flash of jealousy. She's rampantly Scottish, wearing a tartan skirt with a jacket the color of purple heather.

She's also twenty years younger than me, and she'll be at Greg's side during the negotiations. We crossed paths before my retirement, and I did not enjoy the experience.

Jude opens the boardroom door and starts to herd people inside. I duck into the restroom quickly to compose myself.

My hazel eyes smile back from the mirror, changing from green to brown in the different light. I do a quick visual check. Hair's all good. I reapply coral lipstick and conclude that I'll just have to put up with the deep laughter lines. Evidence of a life well lived. I adjust my jacket and smooth it over my hips.

Just as Frances Campbell walks in.

"You look great, Maggie." Her smile doesn't reach her eyes. "That lipstick really suits your mature skin."

I bite back a retort, choosing my words with care. "See you in there, Frances."

I slip back into the conference room as Jude starts to introduce Greg, the opening speaker from the oil consortium. He's the tallest in the room, slimmer than I remember. His hair is silver-gray now where it used to be deep black. Our team used to tease him about his Elvis Presley looks, and now he's a silver fox. It suits him.

All my senses are aware of him as he taps his papers together, scanning over the main points, readying himself to speak.

After that final meeting in LA, I was sick for months. The days at work were long and tedious, and when the children were asleep, I would find myself gazing at Greg's face on our company website, wondering what might have been if I'd stayed.

I slowly pulled myself together, rationing my fix to once a week, then once a fortnight, gradually weaning off the addiction. After a few months, the ache eased, and I wrapped my love for Greg in memory and tucked it deep inside. When Greg's US team finally disbanded, I heard on the grapevine that he and Rachel had become grandparents and retired to their ranch in Idaho. By then, I was happy in Summerfield, and my feelings for him seemed like another life.

Mike, our team leader, leans over as Greg starts to speak. "Didn't you work for Greg Warren once?"

"It was a long time ago," I whisper back. "I don't know him at all now."

Chapter 3

It's been a long day, and I'm exhausted by the time the conference doors open at 9:00 p.m. I want to catch Greg and at least break the ice, but Mike holds me up.

"Great work today, Maggie. We've certainly missed you. What do you think of this angle for tomorrow?"

His words fade into the background as I see Greg walking out the door, Frances Campbell's hand on his arm in an almost intimate way. I turn back to Mike and try to focus on work again. Once we're done, he points toward the bar.

"Time for a drink?"

Greg is there with a bunch of the delegates, but I can't face him now. I shake my head.

"I've got some calls to make. I'll see you in the morning."

I ride the ancient elevator to the top floor. My American colleagues call this hotel quaint and historic, but to be honest, I'd rather stay at a 'not-quaint-and-not-historic' hotel. Square Cottage has the best of both worlds – character architecture with modern amenities. In my attic room, there's a single bed and a tiny desk with a wooden chair. Never mind: I'm tired, and I can sleep anywhere.

But first, I need to talk.

Samantha, my daughter, is one of my best friends. Born with my blonde hair and the cornflower-blue eyes she and Harry inherited from their Dad, I appreciate her perspective. I walk to the window and look out over the rooftops of the city as I dial. She picks up on the second ring.

"Hi Sam, it's only me. I'm in Edinburgh. Are you free to chat?"

"Just for a minute, Mum, then I'm picking up Luke from the University. How's the conference?"

"Pretty good. Better than my horrid room, anyway. I've got a sloping ceiling, a basic shower wedged in one corner, and it smells musty."

"Yuck, can you change it?"

"I don't think so. The oil companies pay for the best rooms for their delegates. I'm getting the environmental experience here."

"Hope you don't get any nighttime wildlife." She

giggles. "Remember Harry collecting all those little black Edinburgh mice in a shoebox?"

"He dropped that box on your Nan's spotless kitchen floor, and they went everywhere." I laugh as I remember the squeals. "It doesn't matter, though, because they've booked me for three more conferences. It will be enough money to cover the repairs at the cottage and maybe even a vacation."

My pension happily covers my everyday living, but it isn't enough to fund the constant upkeep at Square Cottage or the overseas travel I still crave, especially in the depths of the cold, dark, English winters.

"That's great, Mum. Sorry, but I need to go. Luke's waiting."

"Quick question before you go. There's a guy here, Greg Warren, my first General Manager at Banbury. Did I ever mention him?"

"I was only about seven when we moved, Mum, but I've never heard you mention his name." She pauses, senses something is different. "Is he someone special?"

"No. Yes. Sort of ... No. We just worked on the same team for three years, and now he's here."

"I want to hear all about him, Mum. I'll phone on Sunday for the details. Love you."

I smile as Sam heads off, and for a moment, I sit

on the bed thinking back over the day. Am I wrong to think Greg's glances were anything more than just for a colleague? I get ready for bed and fall asleep to the memory of his smile.

* * *

After an early start, the second day of the conference flies by, although there will be a lot more work to do for the next one. We've hardly scratched the surface of their environmental issues, and resolution is a long way off. But I'm pleased with how the conference has gone, and Mike is too. We're clearing our things up and packing bags, and I know I'm going slowly in the hope of catching Greg before he leaves.

"Want to grab a taxi to the airport with me, Maggie?" Mike asks. "We can go over some of the outstanding agenda items."

I glance over at Greg, but he is deep in discussions with Frances Campbell. He doesn't even look my way. I take a deep breath.

"Sure."

The airport is packed with commuters heading back to London. I deliberately lose Mike after check-in, needing time off from the work chat. But I keep an eye out for Greg, finally catching sight of him ahead of me as we board the plane.

I'm sitting near the back, while he's up front again. Clearly, we're just not meant to be together. I order a gin and tonic and sigh as I take the first sip. Finally, I can relax a little and I'm so looking forward to going back to Square Cottage. I imagine lighting the fire and curling up on the couch, pulling my fluffy throw over me and lying back, listening to the rain on the windows.

The flight is a quick hop, and I make my way to Baggage Claim, only to find that my bag seems to be the only one missing. Just what I need. I'm glad I had that drink on the plane, or I'd be raiding the candy machines. Finally, my bag emerges, and I wheel it out into the almost empty Arrivals area, heading for the train.

"Maggie."

His voice startles me, and I spin around. Greg stands there, bag in hand, a smile on his face.

"Oh!" I can barely breathe.

"Sorry, I didn't mean to make you jump," Greg says gently. He walks closer. "It's just that we didn't get to speak at all this weekend. I wanted to talk, but you were always with your team."

"You were pretty busy too," I manage to say, pulling myself together.

"Are you heading for the train?"

"Um, yes. Heathrow Express to the city, then a train to Oxford. How about you?"

"I'm heading in that direction. Walk with me?"

We wander slowly toward the exit, and for a moment, there's a stilted silence. So many years to catch up on.

Greg clears his throat. "I'm staying in London for other business meetings. I was going to meet my niece, Madison, who's at college studying music here, but she's busy tonight ... I've got two tickets for a concert with the London Philharmonic. Might you be able to go with me?"

His words confuse me in so many ways. "Rachel's not on this trip with you?"

Greg's eyes drop to the floor, and he stands frozen. When he looks up again, his eyes are the haunted gray of a timber wolf.

"Rachel died three years ago. For some reason, I thought you knew."

His words echo in my mind. I have so many questions. "I'm so sorry, Greg. I didn't know."

The lines on his face deepen and we stare at each other. When he breaks the awkward moment, there's a tremble in his voice. I've never heard him so vulnerable before.

"So, will you go to this concert with me, Maggie? You'd be doing me a favor."

The woman I used to be is screaming with glee inside. Yes, go, go! But I know that I'm risking so much. It took me years to get him out of my system before.

It takes everything I have to shake my head.

"I'd love to, Greg, but it would constitute a conflict of interest between our companies. I just can't risk it. I need this job."

He nods. "Ever the professional, Maggie. I understand. I'll leave you to your weekend, then."

Greg walks away down the long corridor, and suddenly I remember seeing him like this back in Los Angeles, the echo of my feelings returning with full force. We're both older now. We're not the same people. He's lost his best friend, his loving wife of many years, and he's probably as lonely as I am.

It's only a concert.

"Greg!" I call after him, hurrying to catch up. "Wait, please."

He turns with a hopeful smile as I reach him.

"I was completely thrown by what you said. Just surprised, I guess. Please forgive me. Going to a concert together can hardly be a conflict of interest, especially if we avoid talking about work. I'd love to go if the offer is still open?"

I know I'm babbling, but now all I want is to spend the evening with him.

"Of course the offer's still open. We can have dinner and go to the concert, and I can have my driver take you back to your home afterward. It will be late, but I hope to make up for it with the experience."

"Sounds marvelous." I smile, my heart skipping a little. Greg takes the handle of my bag, and we walk on together to the Arrivals pick-up area.

A dark blue Mercedes limo with tinted windows is parked out front. A young man in a charcoal suit leaps smartly from the driver's seat and opens the rear door as we approach.

"Good evening, Mr. Warren. Good evening, ma'am." He takes my bag.

"Evening, Jason."

I try not to act surprised at this first-class attention, but clearly, Greg Warren has moved up in the world since I knew him years ago. He offers me his hand to help me slide into the limo.

"Thank you." I can't help but tease him. "Is this what they provide for retired oil executives? Where's the little flag for the front?"

Greg grins as we settle into the deep midnight-blue leather interior. It's spacious, with fresh flowers and a mini-bar. Greg pulls out a bottle of Tanqueray No.10 gin.

"Your drink of choice, I think?"

"Well remembered."

He mixes the drinks, and I look out the window.

The powerful headlights illuminate the motorway as we drive toward central London. It's a delight to be in such relaxed luxury, compared to the rushed taxi journey of my departure.

Greg leans back and stretches his long legs. I take a sip from my gin. It's perfect, with just the right tang of lemon with the tonic.

"So what's the program for tonight?"

"It begins with Mendelssohn, the Fingal's Cave Overture. Do you know it?"

"Yes, how lovely. Music from home. I haven't heard that in a long time."

"I don't know much about classical music, to be honest. Madison is the expert, but I'm so glad you'll be beside me tonight, Maggie." He has a soft look in his eyes. "Of course, there'll be no discussion about work?"

"Absolutely," I give him a stern look that quickly dissolves into a smile. "We're on opposite sides of the table now, Mr. Warren."

He reaches over for my hand. "But not tonight."

I turn my head away so he can't see my blush, but I leave my hand in his, relishing his warmth.

We talk about old work colleagues and times past as the car speeds into central London.

"I thought we could freshen up and have a bite to eat before the concert," Greg says as we drive through the ever-narrowing streets.

"That's a great idea. I'd love to change my blouse at least."

"You look wonderful." Greg gives my hand a squeeze.

I'm expecting a mid-level place like the one we stayed at in Edinburgh, but we turn into Park Lane and pull up outside an iconic, exclusive hotel. Jason jumps out and opens the door for me, pulling out my bag and handing it to a valet.

Greg takes my arm, and a concierge in top hat and tails opens the door for us.

"Good evening, sir. Good evening, madam. Welcome to the Dorchester."

Chapter 4

I smile at the doorman and walk inside, looking up at the elegant staircase in front of us. I'm suddenly nervous. This is not the kind of place I'm used to, and for a moment, I long to be on a train heading back to my haven of Square Cottage.

I catch a glimpse of the two of us in one of the mirrors. Greg walks tall, every inch belonging among the A-listers who throng the lobby. I try to look like I belong next to him. I take a deep breath and walk up the steps.

Greg escorts me across the spacious reception area, lit with chandeliers and the scent of roses and jasmine in the air. Spectacular flower arrangements stand on antique tables around the hallway. We walk across the expanse of marble floor to the elevators.

"Do you like Chinese food?" Greg asks as the

elevator doors close and we ascend. "The Dorchester has a number of award-winning restaurants. The China Tang has some of the best Cantonese dishes outside China."

"Sounds fantastic." I'm starving, and right now, I could eat anything. I'm happy for him to take the lead. I'm enjoying being looked after for once.

We arrive at Greg's room, and he swipes his key-card and pushes the door, indicating that I should go in first. I feel like a teenager, excited and apprehensive. I smile to myself. Calm down. It's just a concert. Nothing more.

I walk into the warm and sumptuous sitting room of an executive suite, glowing gold and soft green in the light of discreet side lamps. Everything exudes understated luxury.

My bag is next to a side table, and I hold onto the handle like an anchor. Greg walks over to an elaborate, silver ice bucket with a bottle of champagne inside. Two crystal flute glasses wreathed in frosted vapor stand by its side. He carefully lifts the bottle out, studies the label, then unwinds the silver wire, easing out the cork. It's clear he's done this many times, and I enjoy watching him.

"Fabulous personal service in this hotel."

He laughs. "Nothing but the best for you, Maggie." With the faintest pop, the cork is out, and pale gold liquid sparkles into our glasses as he pours. Greg returns the bottle to the ice bucket, takes a glass, and touches it to mine.

"To old friends reunited." His dark eyes meet mine, and a longing rises inside me. It feels like a dream, to be with Greg at the Dorchester, drinking champagne together.

"To us," I answer and we both take a sip. The bubbles fizz on my tongue. Part of me wants to skip the concert and stay right here with Greg. But he looks at his watch.

"We should probably get ready. There's a second bedroom over there if you'd like to freshen up." He points to the other side of the suite.

"I've only got a new blouse and this suit. Is that going to be okay?"

Greg meets my eyes, and I see something in them that I haven't seen for a long time. "You already look fantastic, Maggie."

A blush rises on my cheeks. "I won't be long, then."

I turn away, grab my bag, and go into the second bedroom. It's just as luxurious as the rest of the suite. Putting my champagne glass down on a side table, I sit on a low chair to take off my shoes and stockings. The deep pile carpet feels like velvet beneath my bare feet. I cross to the bathroom, wriggling my toes, giggling a little as I compare this to my bedroom at the conference hotel last night. From the ridiculous to the sublime, indeed.

I undress quickly in the luxurious bathroom and put my black jacket on a hanger, where the steam will freshen it. I have a rapid but refreshing shower with lots of Dorchester spa products, then wrap myself in two huge fluffy towels.

I dress in fresh underwear and clean my teeth. Might as well be ready for anything! I smile as I imagine what Sam would say if she saw me now. I'm behaving like a teenager on a first date. I put on light makeup and brush my hair until it's smooth and shining. It's a relief to wear it loose after two days tied back. I clip it on one side and replace my mundane, black ear studs with tiny, diamond, tear-drop earrings. They're hardly the Dorchester level of expense, but they make me feel like I fit in a little more.

I pull out a soft, ivory, silk blouse. It has a high collar with discrete ruffles down the front and tiny buttons. I bought it in a mad moment when Sam and I were shopping at a sale in a boutique. When I tried it on, I felt like someone from the era of Jane Austen and Mr. Darcy. I just had to buy it, and it travels with me to events like the conference, sealed in its packaging, just in case. Usually, it comes home again, still wrapped, but now I know it's been waiting for tonight.

I put my suit back on again, but it's transformed by the blouse and my earrings … and by the new light in my eyes. I spray a light spritz of perfume and take a deep breath, then step back out to meet Greg.

He has showered and shaved. Under his suit jacket, he's now wearing a pale blue shirt with an open neck. I can smell his fresh cologne.

"You look beautiful," he says, softly. He takes my hand and turns it over, brushing a light kiss across the back as he meets my eyes. My breath catches in my throat and the years fall away. In this unexpected world of luxury, I vow to enjoy my one enchanted evening.

We head downstairs and enter the China Tang restaurant at the Dorchester. We walk past a stunning Art Deco window in celestial blues and into the main dining room. It has rich, gold decor, highlighted with Chinese paintings in discrete alcoves. A young man in a black suit greets us and shows us to a table, whisking away the Reserved sign.

He holds the chair out for me to sit down.

"I hope you don't mind, but I ordered a selection of dim sum when I booked the table, so we don't have to rush," Greg says, as soon as we're seated.

"My kind of thinking."

A waiter makes a specialty green tea at our table, with grated ginger and fresh lemon. A veritable feast arrives on small porcelain dishes. Greg tells me about each dish and why he chose it, clearly experienced in Asian cuisine. It looks and smells wonderful.

"Did you say you live near Oxford now?" Greg offers me a dish.

"Yes, I bought a cottage when we first moved from Scotland. Samantha and Harry grew up in Summerfield. It's a beautiful village with a great school, and a safe, friendly community."

"How are the kids doing now?" Greg uses his chopsticks to skillfully lift a delicate sliver of chicken from a nest of glass noodles.

"Very well. Sam is a writer, married to a professor at Oxford University. Luke, Sam's husband, does research there and I love having them near me. Harry studied Fine Art at Edinburgh University and now travels the world as a photographer, although he's based in Edinburgh when he's back in the country."

"That's fantastic. I imagine life as a single mom couldn't have been easy."

I take a deep breath as I think of the highs and lows of the last twenty years. "Who said life was meant to be easy?" I smile, and he meets my eyes. I know he's thinking of Rachel. "Of course, there have been hard times. But my kids are doing so well, and I love living in Summerfield."

Transparent seafood dumplings arrive, steamed in a bamboo container like a miniature hat box.

"What about your three?" I ask, as I deftly pick one up with my chopsticks. "How are they doing?"

"Susan, our eldest, went to UCLA, then she worked in the Bay area in a tech company and married the CEO of a start-up. She's bringing up my two granddaughters, Skylar and Shelby."

"I can see you with grandchildren. How old are they?"

"Sky's eight and Shelby's six. They call me Pops." Greg smiles with pride. "I'll see them on the way home. I fly commercial into San Francisco, go and stay a night or two with them in Palo Alto, then take the Cessna back to Boise."

I raise an eyebrow. "You pilot a Cessna? Wow, is that recent?"

"I got my pilot's license about five years ago." Greg pauses, his eyes focusing into the far distance. "It helps me escape sometimes."

"How about your other two kids?" I ask gently.

"Jenna, my youngest daughter, works on the ranch with me. She's a natural with horses, and we work with close friends who raise organic beef."

"I'd like to hear about that. I have an organic garden and –"

A mobile phone vibrates softly, cutting off my words. Greg puts his hand in his pocket, pulls it out and looks at the screen.

I want him to ignore it. I want him to concentrate on me. Just for one night.

"I'm so sorry, Maggie. I need to take this."

As he leaves, I feel suddenly alone in the dining room among a sea of happy couples. I don't belong here in this finery, and anxiety starts to twist inside.

Chapter 5

I take a deep breath and shake my head. Don't be silly. It's probably work or something important. While I wait, I eat the last tasty seafood dumpling, which was technically his.

Greg returns a few minutes later, sits back down and switches off his phone.

"Sorry, that was Jenna." He takes a small notebook from his top shirt pocket. He always used to carry one there to jot down reminders. He writes in a small, neat script with a slim Montblanc pen as he talks. "She gets worried when I'm away and calls every day about the ranch and the horses. I think she still finds life difficult with her Mom gone. She likes to know where I am and what I'm doing, so she can picture me on my travels. That's what she tells me, anyway."

Sounds like she's way too dependent. But I don't voice my thought. Instead, I give him a mischievous grin. "So what did you tell her?"

Greg smiles and reaches for my hand across the table. "That I've had a hard day at work and I'm having dinner with a colleague, then going to a concert. Any hint that it's a *female* colleague and I'd get the Third Degree when I get home."

He returns the notebook to his pocket and lifts the lid on the dumpling pot. A look of slight disappointment crosses his face when he sees that it's empty. I feel no guilt.

"What about your son? Todd, isn't it?"

His expression darkens. "Yes. Todd's a chef, here in London."

"So you'll get to see him while you're here?"

"No, he's working." Greg's answer is abrupt, and I sense their relationship is uneasy. He checks his watch. "Right, we must go. Your carriage awaits."

We head out of the sparkling lobby into the night. Jason is waiting with the limo and we head for the Royal Festival Hall, the home of the London Philharmonic Orchestra.

As we arrive, the last of the audience hurries in and bells ring in the lobby, signaling five minutes to the start of the performance. We're shown to our seats in an exclusive box with a perfect view of the orchestra. I wonder if Greg appreciates how privileged his lifestyle is. But tonight, I'm happy to enjoy that privilege by his side.

Musicians in evening dress take their places on the stage, fine-tuning strings, blowing softly into horns, tightening a kettledrum with a big key. The strings tune to the second violin, and anticipation builds as the lights fade and the audience quiets down. We applaud the conductor as he comes onstage.

Greg takes my hand, squeezing it gently. I return gentle pressure as a thank you. Two thousand people wait in silence, breathing softly in the vaulted, dark space. Like the orchestra, we watch for the baton to lift us on the opening notes. Then, like a flock of seabirds, we ride the swells into the Hebrides overture.

The time flies by, and I am bereft when it ends. It has been a perfect evening in perfect company. Greg turns to me, his eyes shining as we get up to go.

"What did you think?"

"It was just stunning. Thank you so much for bringing me."

It's a bitterly cold London night outside. The wind chases fallen leaves along the Embankment, and a full, white moon shines above the street lamps. I shiver as a knife-edge gust of wind sweeps along the river.

"How about a walk along the Thames?" Greg takes my hand and tucks it through his arm and into his warm pocket. "We'll be warmer once we get going and Jason can pick us up at the Tower."

I don't want this night to end, so I nod, braving the cold for more time in his company. I can sleep in the back of the limo, after all.

London is so beautiful at night. The city lights are reflected in the Thames, the dark river running out toward the sea. We walk past the Tate Modern Art Museum and the Globe Theater. Greg points out the dramatic silhouette of St. Paul's Cathedral across the river, floodlit against the dark sky. He stops to lean against the railing, but as much as I want to enjoy the night, I can't stop shivering.

"Sorry." My teeth are chattering. "It's so cold. I only took this thin raincoat to Edinburgh. It's fine for airports and taxis, but useless for walks in the wind by the river. It was so mild and wet when I left home. I d-d-don't even have any gloves."

Greg undoes the buttons of his big overcoat. "Your nose has gone blue. I'm sorry. I didn't think it would be this cold. Would you like to wear this or come inside with me?"

He opens his arms, and I walk into them,

shivering as I press against him. He wraps the coat around us both, holding it tight behind my back. His arms are strong, and I can hear his heartbeat. We stand together, and I relish his glorious male scent and faint cologne. I haven't been held like this for so long, and I don't want the moment to end.

I want to look up into his eyes. I want him to kiss me.

"I guess I should be going home." My whisper is faint in the dark.

Greg kisses the top of my head and hugs me tight then pulls away slightly.

"We can walk together inside the coat."

It's hard to walk with my arms around his waist and him holding the coat around us, but it's intimate and funny.

"I feel like a kid in a three-legged race." I giggle. "Paired with a boy who is twice my size, with feet to match."

Greg laughs. "I'm glad it's not icy, or we'd end up in the gutter for sure."

We pause for a moment on Tower Bridge, watching the tide racing powerfully through the pillars below. Then we hurry on, trying not to fall over.

The Tower broods above us, London's medieval past silhouetted against the modern office buildings behind.

The limo is waiting nearby, but Greg and I don't hurry now. We dawdle across the empty parking lot like Siamese twins joined at the hip, reluctant to be parted.

Jason spots us and jumps out to open the rear doors of the limo. Greg releases me from the overcoat and the cold night surrounds me again. I miss his warmth already.

We clamber into the warm cave of the limo.

"My overcoat will always hold the memories of that walk." Greg takes my hand again. "But don't sit over there. Stay by me and keep cozy?"

I scoot over to him and cuddle up as the limo drives back through London toward the Dorchester. I rest my head on his shoulder and enjoy being close to him for just a little longer.

"Jason will drop me off at the hotel and then drive you safely back to Summerfield. Is that okay?"

"Yes, of course." I pause for a moment. There are so many things I want to say, and the Dorchester is only minutes away. "I suppose we'll see each other at the next conference then?"

"I'll be counting the days." Greg's voice is soft, and I hear an echo of my own loneliness there. I have to take this chance, or I'll regret it. After all, we only have one life, and mine is ticking away faster than I'd like. I take a deep breath.

"Do you have anything else booked for the weekend?"

"Just some prep work for next week. Nothing major. I might have a wander around the city."

My heart is racing. "Well, you can say no, of course, and I won't be offended. And maybe it's not a good idea anyway, but perhaps if you can fit it in —"

Greg pulls back and looks me in the eyes. "What are you trying to say, Maggie?"

I blurt it out, ready for his inevitable rejection. "Would you like to stay with me in Summerfield for the weekend? I have a lovely guest room."

Chapter 6

"I'd love to." Greg exhales, and his smile is wide as he leans forward to open the window to the driver's seat. "Change of plan, Jason. We're both going to Summerfield so just pull in at the Dorchester, and I'll duck in and get my things, and then we'll be off again."

"Of course, sir."

I can't help grinning as he leans back and pulls me close.

"I'm so pleased you asked, Maggie. I'm looking forward to spending more time with you."

"No talking about work, though."

"Of course. No conflict of interest here."

Jason pulls in at the Dorchester, and I wait in the limo while Greg grabs his overnight bag. Part of me is wondering what on earth I am getting myself into, but my doubts fade as he emerges from the hotel. It's just two old friends catching up, after all. Although, of course, my heart hopes for more.

The limo drives along the river to Chelsea, passing bridges over the Thames and the tall chimneys of Battersea Power Station, all landmarks of London. I like to visit, but I love to go home.

We settle comfortably, holding hands as the street lights flash across the interior of the car, light, dark, light, dark. We're soon on the motorway, and home is only an hour away.

"We never did get to know each other much when we worked together," Greg says. "Maybe that was for the best, but we can make up for lost time now."

"What would you like to know?"

"Tell me more about your Scottish side."

"I'm named after Margaret, a Scottish queen and saint in the eleventh century. All the women in my family were baptized Margaret, although my Mum was the only one who used the full name. My Grandma was Meg, and I'm Maggie. Is your full name Gregory?"

"No, just Greg. For my Dad's best friend who died in World War Two. Tell me about your cottage. I know I'll see it soon, but there's always a smile in your voice when you talk about it."

"Think about walking down an English country

road with hedgerows on either side into the village of Summerfield. Past The Potlatch Inn on your right, a thatched country pub, and then next to some lilac bushes, a drive with a five-bar gate. Square Cottage is set back from the road, surrounded by a rather wild garden."

"I'm with you," Greg says, eyes closed. "We call it a yard in the US, but it sounds like the total opposite of my ranch yard in Boise. Go on."

"As the name suggests, the cottage is completely square. There are four windows, two up and two down, a wooden door, and one square chimney on the top."

"Roses around the door?"

"Of course, in the summer."

"And are there lots of cottages like that in Summerfield?"

"There are other traditional cottages, but mine is unique. I bought it from a professor back when I started working with your team. He said it was originally an overseer's house for the nearby estate. The deeds date back to 1730, and the professor sold it to me because I loved its past and promised to look after it."

"I love listening to your enthusiasm. Tell me more."

"The cottage has an original Summerfield slate

roof. Not like Welsh slate, but thin slices of stone from a type of round rock called a potlatch."

"Interesting. We use the word potlatch in the US too, but it's a Native American ceremony where people give gifts to family and friends."

"That is a different meaning. Summerfield once had land all around it covered with potlatches the size of soccer balls. Generations ago, when they began to build there, villagers cleared the fields and gathered the potlatches. They covered them with wet soil, and on the first frosty night, the church bells would ring out. Everyone uncovered the stones. Water in the fault lines had frozen, and the stones split open, making slices like a rounded loaf, small, bigger, then small again."

"That's pretty cool. And they used those for roofing?"

"Exactly. My cottage is a prime example. Those tiles can be more valuable than the whole of the building, so some people have stripped them off, sold them and then replaced the roof with a modern equivalent."

"But not you?"

I smile up at him. "Sometimes history is more important than money."

The opening notes of Sting's Fields of Gold drifts from the radio in the front. Greg leans forward and opens the sliding window.

"Can you turn that up a bit please, Jason?" He turns back to me. "This song always makes me think of you, Maggie."

He smoothes my hair gently back from my face and slips an arm around my shoulders. I snuggle closer and lay my tired head on his chest.

Eyes closed, we listen as the song fills the dark of the limo and the world slides by outside. I think back to the years I longed to be in his arms, but we have never been as close as this.

Until tonight.

It's nearing one o'clock in the morning when we finally pull into the driveway of Square Cottage. Jason turns off the engine.

Greg steps out of the car and, in his gentlemanly fashion, offers a hand to help me out. I don't need it, but I take his hand, anyway.

He stretches and looks up at the cottage. I try to see it with his eyes, hoping that he will like it. He turns with a grin.

"It's just as you described it. Like a cottage teapot. So quaint."

I make a mock grimace at his American attitude, and we laugh together. There are so many cultural differences between us, but it doesn't matter now.

Jason puts the bags by the door and heads back to London, arranging to pick up Greg again on Sunday afternoon. We have the whole weekend together. I unlock the door and step inside, the welcome smell of dried roses in the air, with a hint of the wood smoke from my fire last week.

"Welcome to Square Cottage." I sweep my arm in a regal way to welcome him inside. He ducks his tall frame a little and steps in through the doorway. "I'll show you around tomorrow, but for now, we are way past bedtime."

Greg yawns. "Agreed."

I walk up the wooden staircase, keenly aware of how tiny the space is compared to the Dorchester. But it's my home, and I know he will respect that.

"The bathroom is here. Smaller than Americans are used to, of course."

Greg pokes his head around the door. "That'll do just fine."

"And here's your room. It used to be Samantha's, so it's not especially masculine." I notice anew the dusky rose wallpaper with butterfly silhouettes.

"I love it, Maggie. You have a beautiful home."

Now that he's here, I'm not quite sure what to do. I fluff the pillows.

"Extra blankets are in this closet, and fresh towels are in the bathroom. Would you like tea?"

He gives a tired smile. "Do you have peppermint?"

"I do. Why don't you settle in and I'll bring it up in a minute or two."

Downstairs in the kitchen, I try to calm my nerves with routine tasks. I put the kettle on the stove and look around Square Cottage. It feels like a dear friend, saying, 'So happy you're back safely.'

The kettle whistles and I pour boiling water onto peppermint teabags in two china mugs and carry them up. I tap on Greg's door. He opens it, his shirt now untucked and the top buttons undone.

Suddenly, the landing feels intimate.

I clear my throat. "Is there anything else you need?"

He steps out of the room and stands close to me. I can feel his warmth, and I want his arms around me again.

"Thank you for tonight, Maggie. It's been a wonderful evening, and I can't tell you how much I've enjoyed your company."

He leans toward me. All I have to do is look up and meet his eyes.

Chapter 7

I take a deep breath and step back, holding the mugs of tea between us like armor across my chest. My head is spinning a little, from tiredness, from excitement. It's too much, too soon. I want to sleep and imprint this day into my memory.

"I had a fantastic time." I hand him the tea. "I'll see you in the morning. Goodnight, Greg."

He steps back into his room, watching me as I walk down the short hallway to my bedroom.

"Goodnight, Maggie."

His whisper stays with me as I slip into bed and sleep.

* * *

When I drift awake the next morning, my first thought is that he is next door. I stifle a giggle into my pillow. Greg Warren. So close.

But I'm not quite ready to get up yet. I want to savor the memories of last night, remembering my hand in his as the music soared around us. The drive back as we began to share memories of the past.

Perhaps it's time to make some new memories.

I slide out of my antique brass bed and reach for my dressing gown. This room can be chilly in the mornings because of the wide windows, but I love looking out onto the fields. From here I can watch the horses running across the meadow or the rain sweeping across the hills and wonder at the spectacular sunsets.

This is my haven.

Sam and I sit here drinking tea and reading sometimes when she comes over. I imagine her squeal of excitement if she knew I had a man here. I giggle like a schoolgirl, my hand over my mouth in case Greg hears me. I head into the en suite and shower quickly, dressing in casual jeans and a sweater.

The sound of the shower comes from the guest bathroom, and I try not to imagine Greg in there as I hurry past. I go down to the kitchen and prepare coffee, looking out as my garden robin sings on the bushes outside.

Footsteps sound on the stairs and then Greg walks into the kitchen. He fills the space with his energy, and he looks handsome in comfortable blue jeans with a light green turtleneck.

"Umm. I smell coffee. Yes, please."

"Still black, no sugar?"

He smiles. "You remembered."

I hand him a mug of steaming black and take a sip of my milkier brew.

"Did you sleep well?"

He sits down at the broad wooden kitchen table, his legs stretched out in front of him.

"Yes, so much better than I did in those city hotels. It's quiet like this at home in Idaho, and I drifted right off. I did hear the rooster crowing this morning, though."

"Sorry, that's our 5:00 a.m. alarm--one of the disadvantages of living next door to Selena's free-range chickens. Did you go back to sleep?"

"Surprisingly, I did."

He takes the proffered mug of coffee and takes a sip.

"Perfect."

I bustle about preparing scrambled eggs on local artisan bread, trying to decide what to show him first. There are so many things I love about living here, and I want him to have a wonderful experience.

Then I remember what we both love most.

"I know you're more used to riding on the ranch, but would you like to ride English style? It's going to be a glorious day, and the hills around here are really something."

I put the plate of eggs in front of him.

"I'd love that, Maggie. My brain is filled with business and the fresh air would clear it out."

He dives in with a hearty appetite, and I sit down next to him to eat. It's strange to have a man in the kitchen. I'm used to independence and having my own space after so long alone.

"I'll phone Clair at the stables and see if there's a horse big enough for you. I go out hacking with her, but I think you just call it riding in the US."

"I'd like that, but I don't have any gear with me."

"If you have a credit card handy, we can fix that. Summerfield has an old hardware store that's now an equestrian boutique. You could buy jodhpurs there, and Clair keeps riding helmets for students."

Not that I want to take Greg anywhere near Cilla Bartlett-Brown, but we'll have to go there, in order to get what Greg needs. I run back upstairs and call Clair while Greg finishes up.

"Should I ask who he is?" Her cheery voice perks up, as I ask if she has a spare horse. "Someone special, Maggie?"

"Just a friend."

"He can ride Russ, Dad's horse. He's got a touch of arthritis, but he'll be fine on a warm day like this."

"Great. We'll be along later."

Back downstairs, Greg is cleaning up and looking out the window. The robin is still hopping around in the bush. The winter sun brightens the colors of the leaves around him.

"There is a horse for you. Nothing too exciting, but at least we can ride together."

We pull on winter coats and head out into the village. I see it with new eyes as we walk, our breath frosting in the air.

"Summerfield was built around what was once a side road for farm carts heading into Oxford to sell produce."

"How did the village get its name?" Greg asks, looking around at the different styles of architecture as we walk up the hill past The Potlatch Inn.

"The land around here all belongs to the Church of England or to the duke's estate. The people who lived here were agricultural workers. In 1850, the duke gave a big piece of land to the Parish Council, so that the village could play cricket against his Woodstock team." I point it out as we walk past. "But the land has drainage problems, and they can only play in the summer; hence, Summerfield."

We walk past the school and the stone market cross, where local vendors chat as they set up their stalls.

"We have a Farmers' Market on Saturday mornings. It's great for cheeses and local meats. I grow my own vegetables, but there are always plenty here."

Greg turns to me. "It's amazing, Maggie. So different from my life on the ranch in Idaho. But I can see that it suits you."

We walk past a row of independent shops and pause at the door of Cilla Bartlett-Brown's equestrian boutique. The huge gold letters, CB-B, are emblazoned in a shield over the door.

The window is full of rosettes, with one exquisite dressage bridle displayed attractively on a stand. As much as Cilla winds me up with her upper-class airs, she certainly has great taste.

"Maggie!"

The voice makes me turn. It's Ellen, a teacher from the school brandishing a donation form. I don't want her gossiping about Greg. He has his hand on the door to the boutique, ready to go in.

"Why don't you get started without me? I'll only be a minute."

Greg nods. "Credit card ready to go. Time to support the local economy." He grins and steps inside, and I turn to talk to Ellen.

By the time I've extricated myself, it's been almost fifteen minutes. Finally, I push open the door and enter the boutique.

As my eyes adjust from the sun outside, I see Greg standing with his legs apart in front of a full-length mirror. Kneeling in front of him, her hand on his inner thigh and her eyes sparkling with flirtation, is Cilla Bartlett-Brown.

Chapter 8

The bell rings as I enter, and Cilla looks up with a practiced, welcoming smile. Her expression shifts to annoyance when she sees that it's me. There are very few eligible bachelors in town, and she's staking a claim on this one.

"Oh, hello, Maggie." She waves her tape measure dismissively. "I'm doing a private fitting right now. Can you come back later?"

Greg has clearly not mentioned that he's staying with me. I hesitate at the door, but he turns. His eyes are warm and welcoming.

"I'm staying at Maggie's." Cilla stiffens at his words, but she's all smiles when she looks up at him, patting his thigh as she continues measuring his inside leg.

"Oh, marvelous. Maggie didn't mention she had a guest coming."

Her breezy reply suggests that we're the best of friends who talk all the time. But the truth is that Cilla only acknowledges me because we both help at the Riding for Disabled Children events. Our lives are so different, but we both love to ride. She's an excellent horsewoman and has three fabulous hunters, which she shows in the summer and rides out with the local hunt in the winter. She's divorced, a petite brunette with a neat rider's figure, and the daughter of a local family with lots of inherited money. Although she's in her late forties, she is acting like a debutante right now, touching her hair as she flirts with Greg.

If he were alone, he'd be invited to stay for coffee – and maybe something more – but not with me tagging along. I suppress my jealousy. Greg can flirt as much as he likes.

After all, he's a free man.

"How long are you in town, Greg?" Cilla's voice holds an invitation. "Perhaps you'd like to come and ride over at my estate?"

"I'm only here for the weekend." He looks over at me. "Thanks for the invitation, but I'm spending the whole time with Maggie."

His words warm me inside, and a blush rises on my cheeks. Cilla bustles about, finding Greg appropriate riding clothes, and we eventually emerge from the shop with shopping bags. We walk home in the crisp morning sun, holding hands as we make easy conversation.

Back at the cottage, we change into our riding gear. I put on my usual fawn jodhpurs, white polo shirt and a riding jacket in burnt-ginger tweed. I'm wrestling with my riding boots as Greg walks into the boot room. I glance up. With a gray sweater, immaculately fitted black jodhpurs, and tall black boots, he looks like a mature male model from a classy catalog. I know exactly why Cilla ended up breathless.

"These are a little snug for my liking." He adjusts the jodhpurs. "At home, we just strap on leather chaps over jeans. I feel like a male ballet dancer in these."

"They suit you. You'll fit right into the English countryside here."

Greg stops fidgeting with his clothes and looks at me, tilting his head to one side. "You look just the part, too. You know, you've hardly changed in the years since we worked together." He reaches forward to gently brush a loose strand of hair away from my eyes. I lean toward him, drawn by the shape of his mouth. I want to be in his arms again, but I also want to show him my life and go out into the glorious sun. I look at my watch.

"We'd better be off. Don't want to miss our ride."

We head purposefully out the back door into the sunny autumn day and walk around to the garage. I open the doors.

"What is that?" Greg stares incredulously.

"My perfect car. It's a Fiat 500, the new model."

Greg walks around the tiny car. It's white with a matte black sunroof and black wheels. "What's this?" He points at the thin red line along the side.

"The go-faster racing stripe."

He throws his head back and roars with delight. "We don't even have cars like this in Idaho. It's a dinky toy, not a car, Maggie. How will I get both my legs in?"

I size him up and giggle. "You can't have a limo all the time, Greg. Come on, this will be fun."

Greg opens the door and slides the seat back as far as it will go. He gets in and folds his legs up under his chin, making a huge deal about it as we head down the lane toward the stables.

His banter dies away as he looks out over the fields. Splashes of lime-green sunlight filter through the leaves as we drive the length of an ancient stone wall. It's a beautiful day for a ride.

Ten minutes later, we pull into the stables. Four horses look over stall doors into the yard. Clair comes out of the tack room and waves. She's tall, early twenties, with short curly hair and a wide, friendly smile. She lives here with her grandparents, Ted and May. I've ridden here since Samantha and Harry left home, and Clair is a great instructor.

Greg clambers out of the Fiat, stretching his legs as Clair comes to greet us.

"Welcome to Summerfield Stables." Clair smiles cheerfully and shakes hands with Greg. "Come and see Russ, the horse you'll be riding. He's been excited since I tacked him up. He knows he's going out."

She opens a stall door and leads out a spectacular horse. Seventeen hands, a bright bay, with a little white around the muzzle. His bright, inquisitive eyes look down at us, and I reach up to pat him. His ears flick backward and forward as he takes everything in. He knows me, but Greg is new to him.

"Meet Russet Bramley III, a real gentleman. He was born here, and he's Grandad's special boy. They retired together, although to be honest, neither just wants to sit around in their old age. He'll appreciate the run."

Clair finds a couple of riding helmets for Greg to try, and one fits perfectly. "Could you fetch Bella, please, Maggie? I'll get Greg mounted."

I strap on my helmet and walk to the end stall.

Bella is the gray mare I ride most often, and she looks around from the hayrack with expressive, dark eyes. I slide back the bolt. "Hello, beautiful." Clair has already tacked her up for me, and I slip a slice of apple into her mouth as I stroke her soft nose. "Don't tell anyone about that."

It's wonderful to be here after two days in Edinburgh conference rooms with no windows, and I'm desperate to be out in the fields. I used to ride sport horses when I was younger, but I don't risk falls now. At fifteen hands and with a calm temperament, Bella's the perfect ride for me these days.

I lead her out and feel the warmth in the sun. It's as if we've been given one more beautiful day before the autumn storms roll in. Horseshoes click on the cobbles, and the saddle leather creaks as Ted holds my off-side stirrup to mount.

"Thanks, Ted."

He smiles up at me. "How are Samantha and Harry?"

"Great, although they don't ride much anymore. How is May doing?"

The smile drops from Ted's face. "Not so good right now." He clears his throat and looks over at Greg. "He seems a nice fella."

We watch Clair coach Greg in the outdoor school

area as he tries to sit comfortably in the unusual riding gear. Clair asks if he can rise to the trot. He looks across at me, raising an eyebrow in an unspoken question.

"It's called *posting* in the US," I explain with an encouraging smile.

"Ah, of course." He turns back to Clair. "Yes, I can rise to the trot, although we don't do much of it at home. I walk out with my daughter Jenna on one of her rescue Appaloosas, checking our stock and fences. So, no fancy stuff, please."

Clair promises him a quiet ride and fetches a young chestnut Arabian called Dolly that she's training for a client. She mounts and walks her around the outdoor school as Russ snuffles in Ted's pockets for treats.

"Wish I could go with you on a day like this," Ted says, wistfully, as he pats Russ. "You look after this horse now, young man. They don't make 'em like him anymore."

"I certainly will," Greg replies, and they smile at each other. Two lovely men from two different cultures, yet similar in many ways. Greg is a successful businessman in his sixties, addressed as if he's a stable lad, and I love that he's respectful of Ted, who's in his eighties now. A weathered, old countryman, happy to have been in service to horses his whole life. A quiet success, but a good life by anyone's standards.

"Everyone ready?" Clair calls as she guides her dancing youngster through the gate. "Can you take the key and go first, please, Maggie? Greg in the middle, and I'll be at the back with Dolly here. Let's hope she's less crazy behind Russ. See you later, Grandad."

Ted hands me the massive key to the park gate. It's on a loop of cord that I slip over my head and hang around my neck, tucking the key inside my polo shirt. I walk on with Bella. The rhythmic sound of metal horseshoes on tarmac becomes muffled as we move onto a cart track to the back gate. Rooks call to each other from the beech trees above us, and we ride in golden, dappled light beneath their branches. I breathe the earthy smell of woods, dreaming of the last days of summer.

I turn to look at Greg. He's riding more easily now in the Western style, on an English saddle, with long stirrups and both reins in one hand. His face says he's in heaven, like me.

"Different from home?" I call back.

He nods. "And some. But wonderful."

Dolly dances and shies away from shadows. Clair coaxes her along until we reach the enormous gate. I dismount, loop my reins over one arm, and insert the big iron key into the lock. The gate swings wide for the others to pass through, then I lead Bella after them and lock it again. Putting the cord back over my head, I mount from a stone post by the gate and trot Bella to catch up.

"Grandad's the last of the estate coachmen," Clair tells Greg as he rides beside her. "When he was Head Groom, he drove the carriage for the family and visitors. Now, of course, they have a pool of cars, a Bentley, a Rolls-Royce and several Range Rovers. The old ways are disappearing."

Suddenly, we're out of the tunnel of trees. The vista of green parkland opens before us.

"Incredible." Greg reins in and gazes down the hill to where the lake curves around the valley and reflects a perfect blue sky. "So many kinds of trees."

I'm thrilled with his appreciation. "This was all planted back in the eighteenth century." I point out over the landscape. "They diverted the river there to create the lake."

We walk the horses around the high perimeter track where every turn reveals a new and spectacular landscape. Clair asks us to wait as she puts her young horse into a collected trot and then a gentle canter. Bella flicks at flies with her tail, while Clair goes back over the places where the filly explodes like a firecracker. Watching her in motion is beautiful.

Greg shifts a little, rubbing at his legs.

"How are you doing?" I ask. "Enjoying the view more than the saddle?"

"I guess it just uses different muscles." He stands up in his stirrups and stretches. "A Western saddle is designed to support the rider for several hours, sometimes even days. So this is different from back home. But Jenna would love this place. I'll have to bring her one day."

Clair waves us on from the other end of the long, grassy track.

"Would you like to canter with Russ?" I ask. "You could hold onto his mane and stand up. If you keep him behind Bella, we can go to the end of this stretch. Or not. Either is fine, you choose."

"I'd like to try a canter." Greg rubs the horse's neck. "I think Russ would too."

Russet Bramley III is looking rather lively, so I urge Bella into a steady trot, then a slow canter. I love her smooth gait, and can easily check on Russ and Greg over my shoulder. We're both beaming with pleasure as we pull up next to Clair.

"How was it?" She's all smiles.

"Great!" Greg pats Russ's neck, and we turn for home, walking three abreast as Clair talks more about the stables.

"We're lucky to be able to ride in the park. There

are only three keys to the gate now, and I have access because of Grandad. Sadly, it will all stop when he's gone."

Greg frowns. "Why is that?"

"Grandad has a tied lease because of his long service. After fifty years, the cottage, stable and fields all revert to the estate. That's next year and we're anxious about it. I'm trying to obtain a loan to buy the lease, but it may be out of my reach. There's even talk of building executive homes on the site."

I understand the economic reality of development in the area, but I hope that the stables can find another way. I hate to think of never being able to ride here again.

"I'm so sorry," Greg says. "It sounds like the end of an era. This was a real privilege, like stepping back into another century."

"Yes, but with a lovely hot shower at the end of it!" Clair jokes, but I sense her unease about the future. I know Ted is worried about her and what will become of the horses. She smiles, brushing away the worrisome thoughts. "Things will work out, I'm sure. Let's get these three home."

Back in the yard, we dismount and take off the saddles. Clair puts head collars on Bella and Russ and sponges them off with cool water. I wash Bella's bit, and we feed the horses treats of apples and carrots. Russ sticks his nose in the air, trying to avoid the fly hood Clair attempts to put on him.

"Stop it, Russ." She leans in to stroke him. "There are still flies around. If you don't have it on, they'll get in your ears and drive you crazy."

Greg and I lean next to each other on the top gate as Clair leads the horses down to the bottom field. As soon as she releases them, Russ gets down and rolls on one side. He scratches his itchy back on the grass, then stands up and gives a big shake. Bella goes next, rolling on one side, standing up, then repeating on the other side while the filly watches.

Then Dolly tries to follow their example but rolls from side to side, her legs straight up in the air. She's still a baby, still learning. She stands and shakes like a dog coming out of water, her tail sticking straight up like a flag. She gallops madly around the field. Greg and I laugh together as we watch her run.

When her energy drops, she moves quietly to join Bella and Russ in the shade by the water trough. Clair comes back up the hill and padlocks the gates behind her. There's a quiet calm that comes from being with animals and riding out together, and I'm happy to share it with Greg. He turns to me as the sun begins to set, turning the sky a dusky pink.

"That was wonderful, Maggie. It's not Idaho, but I loved experiencing it with you."

His words warm my heart, but they are a warning too. I'm aware that Greg belongs in the wild expanse of the American West, not here in the quaint green hills of England.

He will go home. This weekend cannot last forever.

Chapter 9

By the time we get back to the cottage, it's dark, and stars fill the night sky. We're both starving from the fresh air, and I make us a quick pasta dinner, pulling out a bottle of Chianti that Harry brought over one Christmas. I've been saving it for a special occasion, and this seems like the right time. We sit by the fire and laugh about the ride, and I'm so happy to have made new memories with Greg. The cottage is warmer with him inside.

I look out the window and see a high moon, and stars like hard diamonds against the black.

"It's a potlatch night, Greg. Near to freezing. There's something you might like to see. They may not be there, of course, but if they are, it would be extraordinary."

"I'm intrigued." Greg pulls me in for a hug. "I'd love to see more of your world."

We pull on coats and scarves and head out into the night. I put one finger to my lips and motion Greg to follow me. Silently, we move up the garden path toward the back wall that overlooks the fields. Our breath hangs in the air. I pause in the black and white moon shadows under the apple tree.

"The most unusual animals around here are the brown hares," I whisper. "They're bigger than rabbits, have enormous ears and can sprint at incredible speeds. They don't dig burrows, and they stand up on their hind legs, always alert, on the lookout for predators. They're hardly ever seen, but sometimes on freezing nights like this, they come to this field to feed."

We crouch low, creep to the stone wall, and in slow motion, raise our heads.

Three adult brown hares stand motionless on their hind legs, ears and eyes totally focused on where we are. Huge moon shadows stretch across the grass in front of them. I hold my breath, catching Greg's hand in mine, sharing a moment rarely seen.

Suddenly one of the hares springs high into the air and takes off, zigzagging through the patches of moonlit grass. The other two follow in an instant, and they all disappear into Potlatch Wood.

Greg stands upright to look over the now empty field. "That was incredible."

"I'm so glad you saw them." I stand up beside him. "Sam and Harry have hidden with me on nights like this. If the wind's in the right direction and they don't sense us, they box and dance. A moonlight ballet."

"I'd like to see that sometime." Greg's voice is soft, and he moves closer, gently wrapping his arms around me as if I might run like a hare at a sudden movement. He draws me slowly against his strong body, and I relax. It feels right to be here with him. I don't want this night to end.

"Maggie." He whispers into my hair, and I feel the heat of his breath. "There were times in the past when you were so near, and I wanted to hold you like this. But I was married then, and I just had to get away fast. I'm so glad we can be together like this now."

His words thrill me. I remember times when my passion for him was so great, I too had to run away before anyone saw it. It's such a relief to realize now that he felt the same way.

Greg tilts my face up with a gentle hand. In the moonlight and the shadows of my beloved garden, I'm as close as it is possible to be to the only man I've ever wanted like this. My secret love wakens inside again, and I see my longing mirrored in his eyes.

He leans down, and his warm mouth touches mine. My eyes drift closed. With the kiss, a flame flickers between us, like long ago in Los Angeles, when we said goodbye.

He kisses me passionately, and I know I belong in his arms. He shelters and protects me, and we lose ourselves deep in a kiss that feels so right.

I pull away a little, wanting to look at him. I stroke his face, my fingertips etching his jawline, touching his lips. "I can't believe you're here," I whisper.

"This is real, Maggie, and you're not getting away from me this time." He pulls me back into him with the red, wooly scarf around my neck. We kiss again, and this time, his mouth feels more familiar, like coming home.

His dear face is so close, but anxiety suddenly overwhelms me. I pull away. "It wasn't my intent to bring you out here to kiss you."

"Maggie," he says, cupping my cheek, his hand warm against my cool skin. "It was *absolutely* my intent to come out in case there was a chance to kiss you."

I giggle, and together we walk back to the cottage, the night air cool around us. It's been a magical day, and I push aside thoughts of what must happen when he leaves.

* * *

I wake next morning to a blustery wind buffeting the cottage. I lie in bed for a minute, listening to the slates shifting on the roof, hoping that none will come off in the storm. As much as I love Square Cottage, the upkeep requires a constant stream of money, and roof repairs are among the most expensive. I hear Greg moving in the room next door and jump out of bed, eager to spend as much time together as we can before he heads back to London.

We have breakfast together, hands touching as we pass the coffee pot. As I wash up, Greg wraps his arms around my waist and kisses my neck. I lean back against him.

"You make some mean eggs, Maggie. How about I take you out for lunch?"

"Sounds like a plan. Anywhere you'd like to go?"

"I'd love to see Blenheim Palace again. I haven't been for probably thirty years."

"The Orangery there does a lovely British Sunday roast."

"Perfect."

On the way out to the car, I take Greg through the garden. An ancient Peace Rose grows up by the front door. The stem and roots have grown into all the gaps between the stones, up the side, and over the top of the door.

"It's dormant for winter, but in the summer, it has huge ivory blossoms tinged with rose pink. The bees love it. It only lasts a day, but it has an intoxicating scent, and I make potpourri with the fallen petals."

Greg smiles at my enthusiasm. "I hope to see it blooming next summer." My grin widens at his words.

We drive to Blenheim Palace and enter the grounds through the archway from Woodstock. Beech trees gleam gold and green, their leaves always the last to fall in autumn. The lake reflects a pastel blue sky, and we can see people crossing the elegant stone bridge as they walk to the monument on the hill. Heading toward the palace are young parents with babies in buggies and grandparents as outriders to clear the way. Kids and dogs chase through fallen leaves, and high above us, a buzzard drifts in full circles.

"It's wonderful to see it all again." Greg turns to me. "Especially with you."

We walk together through the grounds. A heron darts down to the lakeside, swooping in to catch a fish. Birdsong fills the air as we kick through crisp autumn leaves, holding hands and talking about people we once knew. But time is slipping through our fingers and Greg glances at his watch as we head back to The Orangery for lunch.

"Do you mind if I text Jason, Maggie? He can pick me up here, so we don't have to hurry our meal. I do have to get some work done tonight back in London."

The autumn cold seeps into my skin at his words. I don't want him to go. "Of course."

Greg sends a text, and we walk on to The Orangery restaurant, which overlooks the private Italian gardens. The sound of trickling water from a fountain fills the air. Small palm trees provide privacy for the exclusive tables, each topped by a tiny bud vase containing a perfect yellow rose.

We order roast lamb and a bottle of Argentinian Merlot. I take a sip of the fruity red wine and point out to the gardens.

"Winston Churchill played here when he was a little boy, and he also proposed to the love of his life, Clementine, here."

Greg raises his glass. "To love and life."

I share the toast and we both take a sip. Greg's expression turns serious. "Do you mind me asking about your first marriage, Maggie? You haven't told me what happened."

"It feels like ancient history now, to be honest. We were married for twelve years, most of them happy. But we married young, and it was the first serious relationship for both of us. Of course, falling in love was very romantic, but our folks--his particularly--said it wasn't an appropriate match."

"Why didn't they approve?"

"Class differences don't matter so much in America, but I come from a working-class family. My Dad worked as a carpenter at the docks in Leith. Grandad was a soldier with one of the Scottish regiments." I smile a little, thinking back. "Duncan's ancestors were the lairds of a castle near Aberdeen, so he was expected to marry someone landed or titled. His parents opposed the marriage and didn't come to our civil wedding in Edinburgh, but we were certain about each other in those days, happy just to be together. We both earned law degrees, found jobs, and were happy. Samantha and Harry came along, and everything was great for ten years."

I gaze into the rich, red depths of my wine glass. Time has passed, but I still remember the pain of those days. My heart beats faster. I wonder how much to tell him, how much I can even share without tears welling up.

"Duncan's father died, and Duncan became the Laird and said we had to move north. His mother needed help to develop tourism at the castle to pay for the upkeep. He also wanted more children."

"And you didn't?"

"Sam and Harry are more than enough for me, and I wanted a career as well."

"I can understand that," Greg nods. "I love my kids, too, but I couldn't live without my work. How did it end?"

"We had two years of conflict before we got divorced. The kids stayed with me, and there were some hard times, but I've never regretted what happened. I wouldn't have had Sam and Harry without Duncan, after all."

"Did he marry again?"

"Yes, Fiona. She was a better match in his mother's eyes because she's a distant descendant of royalty. They've been together ever since and had four children. Duncan is a patriarch with six kids, and Sam and Harry have younger siblings, whom they adore." I smile at Greg. "Life has a way of working out, doesn't it."

"You've made it work, Maggie. You clearly did an incredible job juggling your kids and your career. I admire that about you." He pauses. "Perhaps I put my work ahead of my family too much. Rachel certainly thought so."

I think back to one Christmas Eve when Greg worked our team late into the night. Thankfully, the kids stayed with Duncan that year, but I still remember Greg's workaholism, his focused concentration on winning. I take another sip of my wine.

"Has that changed at all?"

"I still like to win, Maggie." His gray wolf eyes harden, and I see the Greg Warren that I used to know, the man who would steamroll those who stood against him. The man who is my opposition to the environmental project. I take a deep breath as I realize how conflicted our interests are, how deeply we differ in our world view. We shouldn't even be seeing each other outside of the project.

"But we said we wouldn't talk about work this weekend." Greg finishes his glass of wine and looks at his watch, his demeanor shifting back into that of the international businessman. I feel a twinge of anger at myself for letting him get close when I know he will only walk away.

A waiter comes over. "Excuse me sir, but your chauffeur has arrived."

Greg nods. "Thank you. Please tell him I'll be there in a few minutes."

We walk out together past the gardens, and Greg pauses in the dappled shade of a chestnut tree. There's a sudden distance between us, and the autumn day feels colder now. He takes my hand and leans in, kissing me on the cheek. His lips linger, and I want to turn my head toward him. I want his mouth on mine again.

But we come from different worlds, and he has to return to his.

I take a step back, the distance between us suddenly so much wider. "It's been lovely to have you here this weekend."

"Thanks for a fantastic time, Maggie. You have a beautiful home." Greg takes a step toward the car, and I can see that he wants to go. "I'll email you."

He gets in, and the car pulls away. I raise my hand to wave, but he doesn't turn. His head bends to his phone as he dives straight back into work again. I fight back the tears as the car turns the corner. How can I have been so stupid? Greg Warren might enjoy a weekend dalliance, but now I am out of sight, out of mind as he focuses on what is truly important to him. His work.

I wipe my eyes and take a deep breath. I'm fine on my own. I always have been. I don't need him, anyway.

Chapter 10

By the time I get back to Square Cottage, I've pushed Greg back into the past where he belongs. I probably won't even be needed for the next Edinburgh meeting, so I might never see him again. The wind has died down a little now, but it was so strong earlier that I know there will be cleaning up to do in the garden. Perfect for taking my mind off things.

I park the car and head out into the front garden with a green sack. As I pick up some of the fallen twigs and brush up the leaves, a sound startles me.

The sliding rasp of stone against stone.

A slate tile drops down from the roof and falls onto the path, cracking down the middle. Another one tumbles after it. I gather up the pieces and look up at the corner of the cottage. My heart is heavy, because this is going to cost me the little savings I have left.

Purple clouds fill the sky above, and I hear the sound of distant thunder. Today started so well, and now everything looks so dark.

A drop of rain falls on my face. The wind whips my coat around me. Another storm will tear more slates off, and I envision my bank balance dwindling as winter approaches. I have to get this fixed. Everything else will have to wait.

I can't do anything tonight, though. Might as well have a long soak in the bath with a book and a glass of wine and try not to think about Greg.

My phone pings as I walk inside.

An incoming email. With his name on it. My heart pounds and I can't help the grin that spreads across my face. He hasn't forgotten me after all. I sit down at the kitchen table and open the email.

Hi Maggie,

I'm back at the Dorchester and just wanted to say thanks for a great weekend. I enjoyed our ride, and I'd like to repay the favor. Would you come to Boise and ride Western style on my ranch?

I've attached my travel schedule before the second environmental conference in Edinburgh. Do any dates fit? I'd like to show you some of my country.

Greg

I put down the phone, my head reeling with possibilities. Yes, of course, I want to jump on a plane and see him again against the backdrop of the Idaho landscape. I want to ride on his ranch and be in his arms again.

But the cost of the flight is impossible now. He hasn't even considered that. It's just not in his reality to worry about money.

I can't go. It's probably for the best, anyway.

I head upstairs to run a bath, pouring in some of the salts that Sam bought for me last birthday. The smell of lavender fills the air, and I start to relax. It's good to know that he wants to see me again. I'm itching to email him back, but instead, I sit on the edge of the bath and call my daughter.

"Hi, Mum." Sam's voice is bright as she picks up. "I wondered when you'd call. I was thinking about you in Edinburgh last week. How was the conference after that awful hotel?"

"It went well in the end. Hopefully, they'll want me again." I pause, searching for the right words. "Remember that old friend I mentioned, Greg Warren? We went to a concert in London on Friday night. Then he came to stay for the weekend."

There's silence for a moment, and I can almost hear Sam's mind whirring. This is not like me at all.

"That's amazing, Mum. Did you have fun?" She pauses for a beat. "Is he married?"

"Samantha, honestly!" I laugh, knowing she would never expect me to behave badly. "His wife passed away three years ago. And yes, we did have fun. We went riding with Clair and today we went to Blenheim Palace. Last night we even saw the hares."

"He must be someone special for you to share the hares with him. Is he still there?"

"He had to go back to London, but it was lovely to have him here. We chatted about the old days and we enjoyed riding together. But he lives in Idaho, so I doubt I'll see him again outside of work."

The sound of pots and pans rattling comes over the line, and I imagine Sam in her kitchen, getting things ready for dinner.

"There's a smile in your voice that I haven't heard for a while, Mum. You know I worry about you being on your own. Maybe you should see him again. Ask him out properly."

"Actually ..." I hesitate to tell her. I feel like a teenager.

"What is it?" There's excitement in her voice. "Spill the beans, Mum!"

"He's asked me to visit him at his ranch in Idaho."

"Ooh, that's super exciting. Will you go?"

"I should say no. There's a conflict of interest with work that could cause some trouble. Plus the repairs on the roof need doing, and then there's –"

"Mum, stop. Listen to yourself. Remember when I met Luke and there were so many things that made it hard to be together? You told me to make it work because he made me laugh. He still makes me laugh. You know how happy we are, and I want you to laugh in the same way. Please think about going?"

I smile and trail my fingers in the bathwater. "I'll sleep on it. Can't let Greg think I'm too keen, after all."

"Don't wait too long, Mum. 'Night then. Love you."

* * *

The storm builds in the night, and I wake in the dark as a snarl of wind and bullets of rain pelt the roof. Then I hear the patter of water from the ceiling as the rain finds its way in through the newly formed cracks. I jump out of bed and run downstairs for a bucket and some pans to catch the water. It hasn't leaked before, and I know more slates must have fallen in the night. The bills mount in my head as I place the buckets under the falling water, waiting out the storm and trying to save my carpet from the downpour.

As dawn breaks and I shiver in the gray light of a new day, I know I can't go to America. This last weekend was a wonderful fantasy, but this is my life now. I can't just leave it all and head to Idaho, where I will likely just be hurt, anyway.

I loved Greg so much from a distance, and it hurt for a long time. But when the hope of another partner is gone, there's room for smaller delights: luxuriating in the bath, the song of the robin outside, visiting friends, painting, and writing. I'm free to do whatever I want to do. It's a happy life.

But sometimes a lonely one.

I sigh a little. Everybody faces loneliness in one way or another, but I have grown used to this life over the years. I also need money to be independent, so I can't jeopardize potential work. It's too risky to see Greg again.

I pull out my phone and send him an email before I change my mind.

Hi Greg,

It was great to see you over the weekend. I'm so glad you enjoyed your stay, and thanks for the kind invitation to visit, but I have to decline. I have too much to do here, and I don't want work conflicts to be an issue. Wishing you a safe journey back to the States.

Maggie

I spend the day cleaning up after the storm, trying not to check my phone every five minutes, just in case he replies. Some other cottages have been damaged in the night, and the heritage roofer is booked out, but I convince him to take a look later and give me a quote. If another big storm comes in, it will only get worse.

It's evening before another email arrives.

Dear Maggie,

I'm back home now and riding fences with Jenna tomorrow. She's taking Blue, her Appaloosa stallion, and I ride Ben, a big old gelding. I'll also be wearing my chaps, although I'm keeping the jodhpurs – just in case.

I want to show you my world. We won't talk about work, I promise.

We're flying to an organics show on Monday and Jenna's staying with her aunt. Meet me in Seattle, and I'll fly you back to Boise in my Cessna.

Please take a chance on me?

Greg

* * *

I barely sleep that night, tossing and turning in the bed. I worry about the rain and the roof and think about Greg riding on the meadows of Idaho, his muscular body taut as he turns to smile at me. I remember his arms around me in the moonlight, the way his lips felt against mine.

I want that again. Of course, I do. Don't I deserve to be loved?

For so long, I've been responsible. I've done everything for practical reasons, always saving money to make sure the kids would be okay. But Sam's right. Greg does make me feel different.

Happier.

I haven't felt like this in a long time. I have to take a chance on him. I can get the builder to put a tarpaulin over the roof and nail it down. The slates can wait. I'll find the money some other way.

I pull out my phone and email back.

Dear Greg,

I really do need to practice riding with a Western saddle. I'll see you in Seattle on Monday. I'll send the details once I've booked everything.

Maggie

Chapter 11

The days pass quickly once I book the flight. Sam is just as excited as I am about it, and I have to keep reminding myself not to get too starry-eyed about the future. Greg is still just a friend, and we both have complicated lives, children, and work we're equally passionate about. But I keep grinning to myself, and I can't help but be excited. Greg's Idaho ranch is a long way from Summerfield, and it feels like a real adventure.

On the day of the flight, I shut the door to Square Cottage and look up at the makeshift repairs the builder managed to get done. It will hold for the autumn, but it needs to be properly fixed before the winter sets in. I love my heritage home, but it's certainly more expensive to repair than a modern house. Still, I have no regrets--right now, at least. I can't wait to see Greg again in his own environment.

It's a ten-hour flight from London to Seattle, but I manage to sleep a little, even in Economy, with my knees up to my chest. I'm bubbling with anticipation as we land, and I want to look my best. I clean my teeth, spritz my face with skin freshener, and put on light makeup before joining the line at Passport Control.

I almost dance along the Customs corridor, and I catch my reflection in a mirrored wall. My blonde hair swings loose and shiny, my eyes are bright, and there's no mistaking the happiness in my smile.

I just hope he's waiting.

My heart pounds as the automatic door into Arrivals swings open. I look around at the crowd of smiling faces, children shouting, and hugs of welcome.

Then I spot Greg, his handsome face in a grin as wide as my own as he sees me. He's wearing gray slacks and a tan sweater with a black leather bomber jacket and there's a pilot's bag by his feet. I'm startled by the memory of meeting him for the first time years ago, how my heart leaped even then.

"Hi, Maggie." He pulls me into a close embrace. "I'm so glad you came."

"Me too." It feels easy between us.

"How was your journey?" Greg wheels my

suitcase with one hand and carries his pilot's bag in the other, as we walk together toward the exit.

"Excellent, thank you. Although I expect jet lag will hit me later."

"Don't you worry. I'll keep you awake."

We walk to the terminal for company jets and private pilots. It feels exclusive, and I have the same sense I did in the Dorchester in London. This is not my world, and I am a little uncomfortable, but Greg is in his element. He signs us in and shows me to a waiting area.

"I just need to check fuel and log my flight plan. Hang out here for a minute." He waves to one of the attendants with the confident air of a wealthy businessman used to people doing his bidding. "Have some coffee."

He heads downstairs. I stand at the window and watch as he walks around a small white aircraft, anchored on the tarmac. He checks a list on a clipboard and texts on his mobile, looking competent and confident, as always.

The little plane looks like a friendly cartoon toy from a movie with three white-hooded wheels and a black propeller. The attendant brings me some coffee.

"That's a Cessna 172 Skyhawk," she says, handing me the cup. "If you're flying to Boise today, you might get a view of Mount St. Helens. The photographs on the wall are of the 1980 eruption."

I study them and read the captions, thinking how bizarre it is to have an erupting volcano in North America. Not that I want to think of disaster when I'm about to get into a tiny plane. After a few minutes, Greg comes back.

"Ready for an adventure?"

"Absolutely."

We walk across the tarmac, and he stows my bag on the back seat behind the front passenger seat.

"There's a baggage port at the back, but it's full of irrigation parts for the ranch. I've texted Jenna. She'll be here any minute. Meanwhile, come and look at my baby." Greg walks me around the Cessna, explaining its features and functions. "It was brand new when I trained on it, so I bought it when I got my pilot's license. You get used to handling a particular plane, and I feel comfortable in this one."

"Plenty of leg room this time." Not like my Fiat 500. Greg grins and pats the cowling.

"This is a Lycoming piston engine, with a range of 640 nautical miles. Very reliable and I do the whole flight plan with real-time data via satellite."

He opens the passenger door and offers me his hand to help me climb in, then reaches across to fasten my seat belt. He leans close. I can smell masculine cologne and feel his strong hands adjusting my shoulder straps. He carefully puts my headset on for me, moving the loose hair away from my face with a gentle hand. He leans in and kisses me gently on the lips. It feels so good to be close to him. He kisses me again.

"Dad!"

The sharp interruption comes from the doorway in a voice that could cut ice. A young woman stands there with long black hair, close-fitting black jeans, and a metallic jacket. She has a row of silver studs around each ear. Her strong face is sullen, and I get the feeling that if looks could kill, I'd have a spear in my chest right now.

Greg's face lights up as he turns to her.

"Jenna. Come and meet Maggie, an old friend from England. You remember I had a team in Banbury near Oxford years ago?"

She moves to stand next to him, putting a hand on his arm in clear ownership. She stares at me without a smile.

"I wasn't born when you were in England, Dad."

"Maggie. This is Jenna, my youngest."

"Lovely to meet you, Jenna." She shakes the hand I offer, but her clear gaze is as cold as her hand.

She carelessly throws her backpack on top of my suitcase, and climbs in, clicking her seatbelt. It sounds like handcuffs closing, and I sense her anger through the seat, but Greg seems oblivious.

He climbs into the cockpit and puts on his headset.

"Let's get out of here. Ready for take-off." He alerts air traffic control with his call sign, and soon we're rolling toward the runway. A little thrill of excitement rises inside, and I try to forget the brooding presence behind me as Greg pushes the throttle steadily forward. The plane accelerates. Then suddenly it leaps into the air as if it can't wait to be up and through the clouds. I must have given a little shriek because Greg turns his head and grins.

"Fun, right?" His voice comes through my headset, and I nod enthusiastically. It's pretty amazing to be up here with him.

The city of Seattle drops away below us, and even with the headset, the propeller sounds loud in my ears. Greg points out Lake Washington and Puget Sound, the Space Needle, and the University.

"Fantastic!" I'm eagerly looking from side to side out the window. "One day I'd love to explore Seattle, another one for the Bucket List."

We climb into the blue sky, passing through fluffy clouds. It's a much more physical experience than being on a passenger jet. I can feel the vibrations of the plane, and I'm so close to the outside world.

I look across at Greg, his strong, capable hands on the control yoke, his body relaxed. He clearly loves it up here, and I try to relax into the journey and push aside Jenna's clear resentment from the back.

"How often do you fly?"

"Most weeks, when I'm at the ranch." He indicates an odd-shaped mountain in the cloudy distance. "Look down there. The collapsed side is where the volcano blew out. Since then, Mount St. Helens and Mount Rainier are continuously monitored. We had a 4.3 quake just recently."

Below us, the landscape passes in slow motion with lakes like puddles in a vast wilderness of snow-capped peaks and ravines.

"I had no idea there was so much forest in the Pacific Northwest. It's beautiful."

"Welcome to my world, Maggie."

Greg begins the descent as Boise Tower clears us for landing. We fly in low over yellow-ocher high desert and land, then taxi toward the hanger.

"That was incredible. I thought we might have to do the 'brace, brace' thing."

Greg grins. "It can get bumpy up there, but I'm glad today was smooth for your first visit." The little plane rocks to a halt, and he switches off the engine. "Welcome to Boise."

"Dad, enough with the small talk." Jenna's tone is

all sweetness with her father, but she still won't look at me. "We need to get going. We're meeting Doug and Barb on the way back, remember? I'll get the truck so we can get out of here."

She climbs out the pilot's door, slings her backpack over her shoulder, and strides off. Greg turns to me as she walks away.

"She'll warm up to you, Maggie. I know she will. Just give her a little time." He grabs our bags, and we walk together across the tarmac.

But he doesn't hold my hand this time as he did in Summerfield.

Jenna pulls up in a huge, burgundy Ford Ranger. She and Greg load boxes of irrigation parts into the truck, and she throws my suitcase in after them. The twilight deepens as we drive to Boise Towne Square. I stare out the window, noting the difference in size here. The roads are wider, the cars are bigger. It's so different from my little village of Summerfield. No wonder Greg found it so quaint. We come from such different worlds.

Greg pulls into a downtown diner.

"You'll love Doug and Barb, Maggie. And we'll try to stave off that jet lag."

Part of me just wants to be alone with Greg, but these are his friends, so I try to be enthusiastic. We walk into the diner past a mural of forests with bears and wolves. There are red booths with polished log poles as backs and armrests. It's rustic, for sure, and I'm amazed at Greg's ability to be as comfortable here as at the Dorchester Hotel. Jenna heads straight for the restrooms, her face like thunder.

An older couple sits in one of the booths, and they wave as Greg approaches. He introduces me.

"This is Maggie Stewart, a friend from my time in England. Maggie, these are my good friends, Barbara and Doug Dayley."

Barbara is petite, late-60s, with gray hair in a neat braid down her back. She and Doug are wearing the same denim ranch outfits, and I feel like a tourist in my fancier clothes. Barbara has a brown, weathered face and intuitive eyes, balancing a firm mouth. She looks like someone who smiles a lot, but as she greets me politely, her smile doesn't reach her eyes. As Doug and Greg sit down, she turns to look toward the restroom, anxious about Jenna.

"Welcome to Boise, Maggie." Doug's a big bear of a man, his gray hair held back in a ponytail under a baseball cap. His kind face is like the glow of a log fire. "First trip to the US?"

"I've been to the US before, but this is my first time in Idaho." I smother a yawn. "Please excuse me, it was a long flight."

"Idaho is the Best State in the Union." He raises a

glass of beer and toasts it with Greg. "I hope you're looking forward to having a great time."

The menus arrive and Jenna still hasn't returned.

"It's not high'n'mighty here," Doug says. "But they serve our very own D-Bar organic ribeye steak as a specialty. Best in the State."

I smile at him and look at the menu. "I'm famished. I'd love a steak."

"My Dad and Mom created our ranch," he explains. "Me and my brother Tommy, we worked with them until we finished school, then Tommy went east. He never was a farm boy, and he lives near Boston now. I took over from Dad later, when Barb and I were married. Greg and Rachel bought the ranch next door, and we've been buddies ever since. Of course, I taught Greg all he knows and..." He pauses.

"...still I know nothing." Greg finishes for him, and they both crack up. This is clearly an old joke between them, and I smile to see a side of Greg I've never seen before. Barb leans in.

"Grown men turn into ten-year-olds over a beer!" She pauses. "They're such good friends, but we didn't know you were coming, Maggie. Greg hasn't had anyone over for a long time. What brings you to Boise?"

I'm shocked by her words. Greg clearly hasn't told them anything about me.

"I'm ... just a friend. We worked together years ago and met again at a recent conference. Greg invited me to ride at the ranch."

Barb's gaze is measured. She knows there's something else going on. The restroom door bangs, but it's not Jenna. She's still in there.

"Please excuse Jenna," Barb says. "Her Mom's death hit her hard. She's suspicious of any other women around Greg, even if they're just a friend. Jenna idolizes him, but they clash a lot. I might just go see if she's all right."

Barb heads off to the restroom as the starters arrive and I happily eat jumbo prawns while Greg and Doug discuss the news from the ranch. A few minutes later, Barb emerges, followed by Jenna. She has a face like her father's, which she can hold expressionless, but I can see she's been crying. She slides into the booth and dives into her meal, pointedly ignoring me. I can only hope that she warms up to me. Otherwise, this will be a difficult trip.

The main courses arrive. My organic rib eye, the best steak in the house, is exactly as I like it. Medium rare with fries and a green salad. It looks and smells gorgeous, and my tummy rumbles in anticipation. It's also enormous.

"I'd forgotten that portion sizes are so much bigger in the US."

Greg laughs. "Dig in. I bet you finish it."

The food is amazing, and I relax a little as we eat.

"Greg said that you ride Appaloosas?" I direct the question at Barb and try to include Jenna too.

"We rescue Appaloosas found in the National Forest, don't we, Jenn?" Jenna just nods, unwilling to join the conversation. "We feed them well, give them lots of care, and then retrain them. Appaloosas are fantastic horses for ranch work."

"Jenna's always loved horses," Greg says, in between mouthfuls of his huge steak. "She used to throw everything out of her baby crib, except for the toy horses. When did she first sit on one, Barb? About a year old?"

Barb nods. "And then she never looked back."

"Thanks for that, Dad," says Jenna, grimacing at the baby story.

"I love riding, too." I try to engage her.

She stops eating and looks directly at me. "This isn't England. Things are different here."

I want Greg to come to my rescue, to acknowledge somehow that there's something between us. But he seems oblivious to Jenna's animosity.

Or perhaps she always comes first.

We finish dinner and say goodbye to Doug and Barb. We head north out of Boise, and I drift off to sleep, lulled by the hum of the truck.

I wake as we turn onto a dark roadway that ends in a big yard. Dogs run around barking, and the security lights come on as we enter. Greg swings the truck around to park by a low ranch house.

As soon as he stops, Jenna jumps out.

"I'll feed the dogs." She heads toward the huge, dark shadow of a barn.

I slide out from the front seat of the truck, unused to the height. Greg grabs my bag, and I follow him onto a wide deck. He opens a screen door and walks into a large, open-plan family room with a kitchen and central breakfast bar. This was likely more homey and welcoming when Rachel was alive, but now it feels like something is missing. But I can't deal with anything else now.

"I'm exhausted, Greg. Do you mind if I go up and get ready for bed?" I'm so tired, I can barely stand.

Greg pulls me close to hug me and kisses the top of my head. "Of course, the guest room is upstairs, second left off the landing. I'll come up in a minute with your bag."

I walk up the wide staircase, my eyes almost closed as the jet lag hits me. I stumble along the landing and push open a door.

"You're not allowed in there." The voice is cold. I turn to see Jenna, her eyes blazing with barely restrained anger. "That was my Mom's study."

Chapter 12

"I'm so sorry." I pull the door quickly shut. "Jenna, I –"

She spins on her heel and walks down the stairs. I don't have a chance to speak to her, to apologize. I have no wish to replace Rachel, and suddenly I'm aware of her presence in this house, her place in Greg and Jenna's life. If his daughter is still grieving, is Greg also still thinking of her? Part of me wants to go after Jenna, to talk to her and clear the air, but I'm so tired.

I stumble along the corridor to the next room, clearly the guest room, with a neatly made bed. Greg brings up my bag, but I'm too tired to talk now. I crawl under the covers and, as I fall asleep, I wonder whether Greg is free to love again.

* * *

When I wake in the morning, the sunshine pours in through the drapes. Everything is green and yellow from their abstract pattern. I can hear sounds of movement downstairs and the smell of fresh coffee. Dogs bark outside, and I feel hopeful in the daylight. Everything will be fine. I just need to make friends with Jenna and start over.

I grab a quick shower and dress in jeans and a red sweater and head downstairs to the kitchen. Greg moves expertly around the kitchen, wearing a big blue apron with *The Boss* stenciled on the front in white. He turns as I enter.

"Morning. Did you sleep well?"

"Yes, thanks." I climb onto a stool at the breakfast bar. "Sorry I conked out last night. You understand jet-lag exhaustion."

Greg rolls his eyes. "Don't I ever. Coffee? OJ? I'm making pancakes with bacon, bananas, and maple syrup. An Idaho breakfast for which I am famous."

"Sounds great." I raise an eyebrow. "Nice apron."

"Christmas present from my granddaughters, Skylar and Shelby." He puts oranges through the juicer and pours the fragrant liquid into tall glasses over ice. He adds a pink cocktail umbrella and hands one to me with a flourish. "Coffee coming up."

It's good to see him bustling around the kitchen, flipping pancakes, grilling bacon. The smell fills the kitchen as he serves it up, passing me a bowl of bananas and a jug of maple syrup. Forget the diet. I dive in.

"I did wake in the night. I thought I heard wolves. Was I dreaming?"

Greg shakes his head as he coats his bacon in syrup. "Northern gray wolves are now living in the forest above the Upper Road. They've been extinct in Idaho for over seventy years, but they were re-introduced to Yellowstone in 1995. We have a Wolf Program to bring them back to our National Forests."

"Don't wolves kill cattle?"

"Rarely, except maybe a lone calf once in a while. Some of the ranchers are scare-mongering, saying wolves mean the end of their business, but there's an office in McCall that monitors the wolves 24/7 via radio collars. If they go onto farmland and kill, they're captured and relocated, and the farmer gets compensation. We're hoping that the wolves will rebalance the elk population, which is out of control, damaging too many trees."

"Sounds like a great program. Is it working?" I munch happily on my breakfast, enjoying the sugar rush.

"I think so. The Nez Perce have taken over the Wolf Recovery Program, and it's now one of the most successful in the country."

"Nez Perce?"

"The local Native Americans. Their name for themselves is the *Nimi'ipuu*, which means, *We, the people*. But early French trappers used the term Nez Perce, meaning pierced nose. Not that they ever had pierced noses, so the name was a mistake, but it stuck. After the Indian Wars, the settlers compounded it by building the town of Nez Perce."

"It's such an interesting area."

Greg reaches over and takes my hand. His gray eyes meet mine, and he speaks softly. "I hope to show you much more of it. Would you like to ride this morning? It's the best way to see the ranch."

"There's nothing I'd rather do. Will my English riding gear be OK?"

"Fine for now. We've got some half-chaps and Stetsons in the barn."

"Sounds good." I climb down from my stool, eager to be out riding with him under the sun. "I'll go change."

I run back upstairs just as Greg's phone rings. When I come back down, dressed in tight-fitting British jodhpurs, red sweater, and tall black boots, Jenna is standing in the kitchen wolfing down the leftover pancakes. Greg is still on the phone, his face creased with concern.

I remember that look from projects in the past and a chill runs down my spine.

Jenna is wearing comfortable blue jeans, a checkered, flannel shirt, and scuffed ankle boots. She looks me up and down. Clearly, my British riding gear is alien to her, and I feel every bit the outsider.

"Morning, Jenna."

She turns away and kisses Greg on the cheek as she heads out the door. "Later, Dad."

He cups a hand over the phone. "Jenn, wait up. Something's slipped on the project. I have to get on an emergency call in ten minutes, and it might last a while. Doug and Barb are out for the day. Can you take Maggie on your inspection ride, show her the Lower Valley? Saddle up for her too. She's never ridden Western." Without waiting for her answer, Greg turns to me. "I'm so sorry, Maggie, but I need to do this. Go with Jenna and have a good ride. I'll see you both later."

Without so much as a backward glance, Greg hurries out of the room, resuming his conversation on the phone. Jenna and I stand in the kitchen, an awkward silence between us.

"Come if you want to," Jenna says and walks out the door into the sunlight.

I'm torn. Part of me wants to wait for Greg, chill out here in the farmhouse and not have to face his angry daughter. But the other half of me, the half who watched my own children deal with grief and upset over the years, wants to try with Jenna. If I want to have any chance with Greg, I have to get along with his youngest child. I'm angry at him for putting me in this position, but maybe it's the chance we need to get better acquainted.

I pull on my tweed jacket and follow Jenna to the barn. She's standing by the door, her dark eyes a little surprised to see me follow her. With her raven-black hair and the sun shining on her high cheekbones, she looks as if she belongs out here, part of the land her ancestors came from.

"Come and meet Blue."

For the first time since we met, Jenna's voice is warm, and her smile is real. We both love horses, so perhaps this ride won't be so bad after all.

She swings wide the barn door and makes a clicking sound. The most magnificent stallion I've ever seen paces out. He must be sixteen hands or more, a perfect leopard-spot Appaloosa, jet black with white patterns on his rump and shoulder.

He moves to Jenna and nuzzles her hair as I find myself staring in admiration. Blue is like a mythical horse from legend, beautifully proportioned with a defined muscular body, an arched and sculptured neck, a long mane, and the softest black velvet muzzle. He majestically lowers his head and blows down Jenna's neck, as if talking to her.

"He's unbelievable." My voice is soft, and Jenna smiles slightly, acknowledging this truth.

"Dad and Barb want to me register him, but I won't do it. It would be an insult. He's not just an Appaloosa. He's the Spirit Horse of an Ancient People. He came into my life, and I care for him while he's here. We have pictures of him on our website, and if someone wants a foal, they bring their mare over. If Blue likes her, then she runs with his herd, and they pay a fee if they get a foal. But so far, in eight years, there have been no foals, because he's unique. He's a Spirit Horse. There'll never be another like him."

Jenna turns to the corral, one arm around Blue's neck and indicates five horses standing together in the shade, tails swishing.

"Who do you want to ride? They're all good."

I study the group for a minute or two, then point to a bay mare, the smallest at about fourteen hands.

"How about that one? She looks quiet. Probably best for my first day here."

Jenna hesitates for a split second. There's a flash of something in her eyes, but it passes quickly. "That's Brownie, she'll do."

She leads the mare into the barn and starts to get the tack ready.

"Could you teach me to saddle up?" I ask. "So I can do it myself next time."

Jenna bristles at the words, as if there won't be a next time. "Saddle's too heavy for you to lift. I'll do it for you." She shoulders it easily onto Brownie. She gives me some half-chaps and two Stetsons to try. I stuff my sunglasses in my pocket and copy her, strapping on the leather chaps.

I try on the hats. One of them just about stays on with the cord done up tight. Jenna helps me to mount, adjusting stirrups and checking the cinched girth. She's swift and capable, and her fingers linger on the horse's body. I can see she's more at ease with animals than people.

Or perhaps it's just me.

She puts on her own battered Stetson, her dark hair hanging down in two long braids. She shrugs into an old coat, takes a lariat from a peg, puts it over her head, and hangs the coil across her body. Blue waits perfectly still, and in two leaping steps up the fence rail, Jenna vaults onto his back. She has no saddle, no bridle, not even a head collar.

She sits for a moment, looking like a centaur, melded into her horse. The stallion's perfect black ears flicker backward and forward, hyper-aware.

She wraps one hand into his mane and with a barely perceptible movement, communicates to Blue to walk on.

I click my heels and follow sedately on Brownie, trying to stay calm as I get used to the new horse in a new setting.

Jenna rides ahead, looking around every now and then to check that I'm following. I should be grateful for that, at least. As we move through the paddocks, she starts work, counting steers in the top pasture.

I try and relax into the ride, putting my sunglasses back on and settling the Stetson more firmly on my head. It's fabulous to be out on a horse in this stunning place and Greg's right, the Western saddle is built for comfort.

Although it would have been nice to share this first outing with him.

Never mind. The sky is a sparkling azure, and we ride along the edge of the Payette National Forest between well-tended fields of healthy beef cattle. Jenna sits for several minutes on Blue and watches each herd, listening and observing. She makes an occasional note in a small, spiral-bound notebook she takes from the top pocket of her shirt.

I can see her father in the way she works.

When she's satisfied, she checks the water troughs

and walks Blue on. I stay a little way behind her, preserving the silence. She's clearly happier just being out here, and I feel as if I'm witnessing something spiritual in her rapport with Blue.

I'm more relaxed with Brownie now. One hand on the reins and slight pressure on her neck is all it takes to guide her. I whisper to her quietly as we ride along and enjoy the views.

A little further on, we turn into the forest, and Jenna rides out of sight. My heart beats faster. She wouldn't have left me, would she? I could get lost out here since the ranch is so huge and I haven't been paying attention to where we are. I trot Brownie on and am relieved to see Jenna waiting for us at the next bend.

"You OK?"

I smile, glad she's asked. "Yes, thank you for letting me join you. I'm finding this Western saddle more comfortable than our English ones. I don't think Greg enjoyed his ride with me so much."

Jenna stiffens and looks at me with narrowed eyes. It's clear she didn't know that Greg had ridden with me before.

"Better keep up now. The paths aren't so clear in the forest."

She turns Blue and walks on, then abruptly angles him down a path overshadowed by trees. Brownie and I obediently follow.

Jenna rides faster now and draws further ahead. I kick Brownie gently to catch her up. I hear the sound of rushing water, and the mare pricks up her ears, quickening the pace. Perhaps it's where they stop to have a drink of water on the way home.

We break from the path into a clearing. Jenna and Blue enter the creek and move smoothly across to the other side through the fast-flowing water. The froth of whitewater splashes over rocks, eddying on the other side. The water level only reached the tops of Blue's legs as he crossed, so it should be fine on Brownie.

Jenna sits on Blue, looking back at me, a question in her eyes. A test of horsemanship, perhaps? I've ridden through plenty of water in my time, so I urge Brownie onward.

She hesitates.

I ride with a loose rein and kick her on as I would do Bella at home. Brownie steps into the stream with her ears forward and I hold the saddle horn as the water brushes my expensive boots. I lift them as we go deeper.

Brownie stumbles. She starts to give at the knees.

I shout in alarm, pull her head up and kick frantically. I realize suddenly that she intends to roll.

But it's too late.

The mare drops to her knees in a great splash of

water and starts to tip sideways. Instinctively, I pull my feet out of the stirrups and throw myself away from her.

I gasp at the freezing water, turning from her plunging body and thrashing hooves. The too-big hat falls over my eyes. My sunglasses break as the force of the tumbling creek smashes me against a rock.

I put my hands out to grab something, but the water pounds me. I struggle to stand, desperate for a foot hold on the slippery rocks underneath. The current smacks me into another boulder and I lose my grip. I choke on a mouthful of water. My vision starts to narrow, and the current pulls me under.

Chapter 13

I bob up again in the spinning, rushing torrent, desperate for a way out. Suddenly, I feel the slap of rope on my shoulder.

"Grab it, Maggie!"

Coughing and spluttering, I manage to grab the rope and loop it around me. Jenna slowly hauls me out of the current. When I feel the stream bed beneath my feet, I stumble forward and sit down heavily on the bank. I put my hand up to wipe the water off my cheek. It comes away scarlet with blood.

"I'm so sorry, Maggie." Jenna kneels beside me, one hand on my shoulder. Her eyes are wide. She suddenly looks young and afraid. "Are you all right?" She holds out a folded neckerchief. "I can't phone for an ambulance. There's no reception down here."

I'm winded, breathless. I take some deep breaths to calm myself. Slowly in, slowly out.

I press Jenna's neckerchief against my cheek, mentally scanning my body for injury: arms, legs, fingers, toes, head, neck. Everything seems to be all right. I've fallen off many times before, but not in the past few years. Bella is my safe ride, and right now, I miss her desperately. I miss Summerfield, my home. What am I doing here so far away with a man who can't ignore his work for me, and his daughter who clearly wants me gone?

I shiver violently, as shock sets in. I'm suddenly exhausted.

"We have to get back." I struggle to stand, and Jenna takes my arm, helping me to a tree. I lean against it while she runs to get Brownie. The mare emerges from the water, her saddle askew. She's dripping with water and shakes vigorously. She looks quite pleased with herself. Jenna checks her over, cinches the saddle, then wades into the water to retrieve the hat.

"I should have paid better attention to her behavior." Tears sting my eyes. I'm cold and in pain and I've had enough of this.

"It wasn't your fault." Jenna is sheepish. "Now you need to get back on, so we can ride home. You need to get warm."

I don't think I can manage to get back in that saddle. I shake my head. "I'll walk."

Jenna looks panicked. "It's too far. You can't walk. We have to ride." She pauses. "Or I'll have to go and get Dad to help."

I think of Greg back at the ranch house, leaving me to ride alone with Jenna. I won't give him the satisfaction of rescuing me. The spark of independence gets me going. I'm beginning to stiffen, and it's always better to get right back on the horse.

Jenna helps me climb an outcrop of rock and get mounted again. She swings herself back onto Blue, still holding Brownie's reins.

"I'll lead her if you like. Just hold on to the saddle horn."

Shivering violently, I snatch the reins out of her hand, pull the mare's head around, and give a hard kick. Brownie jumps forward.

"I don't need to be taken home on a leading rein," I snap at Jenna. She's done enough for today. She heads Blue up the narrow track. I fight back the tears as I follow on Brownie. There's a massive scrape on my cheek that's still dripping blood down my face. My nose is swelling and I can feel a black eye developing from the smack against the rock. I'm dazed and miserable.

So much for a happy day's ride out with Greg.

Jenna takes a shortcut across the paddocks, and we emerge at the back of the ranch house next to a wooden staircase. Jenna dismounts and helps me to slide painfully off Brownie.

"These stairs lead up to the deck by the guest room. I'll see to Brownie and Blue, then make you some hot tea. Are you OK to shower?"

I nod, moving gingerly to avoid bumping my scrapes and bruises. I don't want Greg to see me like this, so I head upstairs, soaked and shivering, pulling myself up with the handrail.

When I shut the door of the guest room behind me, I lean against it and stifle a sob. I'm a stupid fool with shattered romantic dreams and a broken, old body. I just want to go home.

I strip off my soggy clothes as fast as my trembling fingers will allow and stand under the hot shower. My head is spinning so I hold onto the wall. I can't risk another fall. Turning slowly under the hot water, I let it massage each part of me again and again until I'm finally warm. I gently wash my hair and rinse my face with handfuls of cooler water to wash away the blood.

Out of the shower, I wrap myself in towels and examine my face in the mirror. The scrape across my left cheek looks like Harry's grazed knee when he fell off his skateboard years ago. There's grit impacted into the skin, and it's seeping droplets of blood. But I don't think my cheekbone is broken. Hopefully, I won't need stitches. However, I'm going to need some painkillers to get through the next day or two.

And as much as I don't want to make a fuss, I need to get to a hospital for a scan. I'm fully aware of people who have falls from horses or when out skiing and seem to be fine, then die a few hours later from some internal injury. It's not exactly the best start to a romantic getaway.

My left eye socket and nose are swelling and bruised. Suddenly, I feel my age, and the thought that Greg could find me attractive now seems impossible.

I tug on a soft sweatshirt and jogging pants just as there's a gentle knock at the door.

"Maggie," Jenna's voice is quiet, contrite. "Here's your tea."

I pull open the door to let her in and then sink down into the easy chair. Her eyes are full of tears as she puts the tea down next to me.

"I'm so sorry you're hurt. Can I get you some painkillers?"

"I need to go to the hospital, just in case anything's damaged." Jenna looks stricken at this, but I see she understands. Horse people know the reality of falls, and she must have had her share. I nod toward my suitcase and a pair of socks on the top. "I could use some help getting those on, though. I can't bend down right now."

"Of course." Jenna crosses to get the socks and lifts my feet, one by one, to put them on. She is gentle, as she would be with a wounded horse.

"Thank you, dear," I say, as I would to Samantha. "You must have been such a help to your Mom."

Jenna looks up at me with the same gray wolf eyes as Greg's, full of conflicted emotion. "Maggie, I'm –"

The door swings open and Greg strides in. Jenna jumps to her feet.

"Hi, guys. I didn't hear you come in. Did you have a good …" He sees the state I'm in, and his face goes white. "Oh no, Maggie. What happened?" He moves swiftly to my side, crouching down, with a hand on my arm.

"Oh, nothing much. I took a tumble off Brownie into the creek." I try to be lighthearted about it, but the pounding in my head is getting worse. "It's fine, I'm sure. But I do need to go to the hospital for a check-up."

Greg rises like an avenging angel and turns on Jenna. She's standing right by the door now, her hand on the latch. She's ready to run.

"Dad, I –"

"You took that mare near water?" Greg's fury drives Jenna out the back door, and her footsteps clatter down the stairs.

Greg leaps to follow her, but then checks himself, turning back to me.

"I'm so sorry, Maggie. I should have been there. I'll take you to the hospital right now and deal with Jenna later." He bends to help me up, and I relax into his embrace. I'm relieved he's taking charge, because I can't cope with anything else today. I lean on him as he puts my warm coat around my shoulders, helps me across the yard and up into his truck.

The ride to the hospital is a blur, but once I get some painkillers, I'm happy to let the doctors do their thing. Greg knows people here, and I'm seen immediately, a whirlwind of scans and tests while I sit in a haze, waiting for it to be over. Everything is fine, and I just want to sleep away the pain.

In the truck on the way home, Greg keeps looking over at me, his face concerned. He reaches out and strokes my arm. I'm enjoying the attention. I just wish it could have been under different circumstances.

"I'm so sorry this happened, Maggie. Brownie is a rescue mare and for some reason, she rolls in water with anyone on her back. Jenna shouldn't have taken you anywhere near the creek. I could never imagine in a million years she'd do something like that."

"You didn't tell her I was coming." A whisper is all I can manage. "You brought a strange woman into her mother's house without telling her. No wonder she was angry."

Greg visibly bristles at this. "It's my house. I can bring whoever I want."

"I can't talk about this now." We pull into the yard. He opens the door for me and helps me toward the house. "I need to lie down before I throw up."

He helps me climb the stairs and into bed, tucking the sheets around me. He adjusts the pillows so that I can recline with no pressure on my face. "I'm going to keep coming in and checking on you, just in case." He bends to kiss my forehead and then pulls my door half-shut as he heads back downstairs.

I'm drifting into sleep as the screen door slams on the back porch.

"How's Maggie?" Jenna's voice is concerned.

"You're very lucky, Jenn, and so is Maggie." Greg's tone is steel-hard. "She could have hit her head and been blinded or even killed. I trusted you to take her out for a quiet ride. What on earth were you up to?"

"She chose to ride Brownie. And I didn't mean for her to be hurt, just get a soaking, to learn what it's like out here. This is not the quaint British countryside."

"Maggie is my guest. I hoped you might like her." His voice is placating.

"She's clearly more than a guest." Jenna's voice is hard now. "You went riding with her in England, but you didn't tell me about that. You betrayed Mom, and now you've brought that woman here to our family home. She doesn't belong here." There's a crash as something is thrown to the floor. Jenna is shouting now. "If you must have another woman, get one who'll be of use to us on the ranch, not some fancy British dame in jodhpurs."

Jenna slams out of the house and, from my window, I see her storm across the yard.

A moment later, she catapults from the barn on Blue. The stallion seems to be roaring, his head back, his mouth wide open. Jenna crouches over his neck, her braids unraveling into a long tangled mane like his. She passes the ranch house and gives a blood-curdling war cry that makes the hair stand up on the back of my neck.

Silence surges back into the quiet yard after she's gone, and I hear the creak of a chair as Greg sits down. I imagine him wanting to go after his daughter. After all, she is his blood, and this is their land. Jenna's right. I don't belong here and there is no hope for Greg and me.

As sleep eases my body into oblivion, I know I need to go home.

Chapter 14

When I wake up, the pounding in my head has stopped, but I can feel every inch of my bruised body. The sound of songbirds comes from outside, and I sense it must be just after dawn. I open my eyes and see Greg sitting by the bedside. Has he been here all night? I half-smile as he looks over, then wince with pain at the movement.

"Hey, gorgeous," Greg says with a smile. Although I must look an absolute wreck, I can see in his eyes that he means it. He takes my hand and kisses it gently. "How are you feeling?"

"Like I've been hit by a truck." I remember Jenna storming off before I slept, and I know I have to leave. Best to get it over with now. "Greg, I –"

"Maggie, please." His words cut me off. "I'm so sorry for what happened. It's as much my fault as

Jenna's that you've been hurt. Please let me make it up to you." He strokes my hair with a gentle hand. "Since I met you again, it's as if I'm thawing from a long winter. I know I haven't handled it so well, but please, give me another chance."

I sigh a little and shift on the bed. Of course, I want to stay, but I don't think I can cope with any more family conflict. "How's Jenna?"

Greg frowns, his expression darkening. "She's with Doug and Barb." He rubs his forehead. "To be honest, she and I clash a lot, but she finds solace with Blue. I love my daughter, but she drives me crazy sometimes."

"She's a lot like you."

He laughs. "Yes, Rachel always said that."

The mention of his wife's name doesn't hurt now. I like that he can be honest with me. Greg stands up.

"I'm going to get you some tea. Then I thought maybe we could start over. I'd love to take you up to my cabin by the lake at McCall, just until you have to go. You can rest, I'll cook for you. There will be no horse riding and no Jenna. Just us."

"No work calls?"

He nods. "I've told everyone I'm off the grid."

"Then yes, I'd love that." I try to sit up. He comes back to the bed and helps me, plumping the pillows behind.

"Just rest now. I'll get your tea and help you pack up. It's only a few hours' drive north to McCall. It's a special place, and I want to share it with you."

By the time I've had tea and breakfast, I'm feeling more human again, and I love having Greg wait on me. It's been a long time since anyone looked after me when I was sick. I'm so used to being on my own, and yet letting go of control feels liberating.

We get into the truck and head north. At first, the road runs through ranches and grasslands with cattle, similar to the D-Bar and Warren ranches. Then it climbs into the mountains through the National Forest. Whitewater tumbles down the mountainside, sparkling in the bright sun. Now and then the road crosses a flat grassy plain with small settlements and grazing cattle. It's peaceful, and I can see why Greg retreats here, away from the business world.

We drive in silence for a while, comfortable in each other's company. After a while, Greg shifts his hands on the wheel and takes a deep breath.

"It feels strange to be taking time off work," he says. "But the truth is, I'm not the high-powered executive anymore, Maggie. I'm meant to be retired and working more on the ranch than in a conference room. I guess I just can't let it go. It's such a part of me."

I smile over at him. "I know exactly how you feel. I struggle with it too. The 'retired' now are people who were often incredibly successful. But who and what are we now? What's our value? We're all trying to redefine ourselves, Greg."

"I think that's part of why I clash with Jenna. She's trying to find her way in the world as a young woman, and I'm trying to find my way as an old man."

I reach over and pat his thigh. "You're not so old."

He grins. "Well, I need to apologize to Jenna, but she also needs to apologize to you."

"In her own time. And just so you know, I hate shouting and open conflict." I pause, thinking of the past. "My Dad was war-damaged. Post-traumatic stress disorder, but back then, of course, they didn't know what it was. There was no understanding or treatment. He drank to shut out the memories of war, and we had to live with that, my Mum, my sister and me. It was frightening, and I don't need any more shouting and anxiety in my life, Greg. I need calm."

"It helps when you tell me stuff like that," Greg says, as we turn around a bend and there's a view of Lake Cascade with its brilliant blue water. "My father's leg was crushed in a logging accident when he was a young man. All his friends went to the war and became heroes, but he was medically unfit to fight, and it left him with a rage against life and a drinking problem, too. So I know what you mean." He glances over at me. "But I don't remember the Maggie Stewart I saw at work being averse to conflict."

"That's different." I smile over at him. "We both still want to win in the business arena."

We laugh together and drive the rest of the way to McCall listening alternately to a track of classical music, Greg's favorite, then country fiddle music.

He groans at my choice. "Is this punishment? Or do you just have terrible taste in music."

"You know you love it, really."

We pass the sign for McCall.

"I went to elementary school here," Greg says. "But there weren't enough kids for a junior high, so they bussed us down to Eagle. I met Doug there, and we both went on to Boise High. He got pushed around one time by some jocks, but I was raised in Northern Idaho, so I knew how to bang a few heads together."

I try to imagine him as a young man. "So you helped Doug out?"

"Yeah, but he helped me too. The more they teased me, the more tongue-tied I got."

I laugh at the thought of Greg Warren being

tongue-tied, but actually, he doesn't say much, unless he's passionate about something. "Doug can talk to anybody. He talked me all the way through junior high and into senior. He met Barb and introduced me to her friend, Rachel. He did most of the talking in our courtship, and we both married our childhood sweethearts."

We pass a sign for Warren Wagon Road, and Greg slowly turns onto it, driving along the lakeshore. There's no tarmac here. I can't help but groan as the bumps jolt through my bruised body.

"You all right?" Greg asks, anxiously.

"I think the painkillers have worn off."

"Not long now."

Minutes later, we pull up at a cabin set back from the lake, a two-story timber building with a long porch on the front. The late sunshine reflects a million sparkles from the Payette Lake. It stretches in every direction, a mirror image of the cobalt-blue sky framed by dark-green conifers which rise to the snow-topped mountains. A pair of cormorants are fishing out on the lake and their calls are the only sound. Sunshine glitters off every ripple. It's stunning, and I long to find a canvas and paint the dynamic colors in hues of blue, yellow and deep reds.

Inside, the cabin is homey and welcoming, with

comfortable couches and bright, rustic colors. There are warm drapes and rugs on the polished wood floors.

Greg opens a bottle of Merlot, letting it breathe as he prepares dinner. The sound of him chopping vegetables comes from the kitchen as I relax on the deck, looking out over the water as the sun goes down. He comes out with a glass of ruby-red wine and places it next to me. Then he gets a blanket, lifts my legs onto a stool and wraps the blanket around me.

"It gets cold as darkness falls," he says, softly.

I look up at him, the strong lines of his face chiseled by the dusky light. "It's beautiful here. Thank you for bringing me."

He leans down to kiss the top of my head. "I only wish I would have thought of it earlier," he says. "I'm going to light the fire, so it's toasty for dinner."

We eat by the window, looking out over the lake. The wood stove doors are open, throwing out warmth and the cheerful light of burning logs. We have fresh trout pate with Melba toast, venison with buttery potatoes, and green beans. Greg mashes the potatoes into the delicious venison gravy for me, and I manage to eat with a teaspoon. We laugh together as he helps me, and it feels natural to be here with him. Perhaps because this tiny cabin is more like Square Cottage and it feels more like home.

Afterwards, we sit together on the deck, the blanket wrapped around us. The stars are so bright here. There's no light pollution, just a forest that goes on for miles and miles in every direction. I relax in his arms, my head on his chest, listening to his heartbeat. A night bird trills, calling to its mate.

Then a lone, gray wolf howls in the silence of the forest.

"There's a pack living close," Greg says as he strokes my hair. "I've grown up with that sound. I miss it in the city."

"You used to live in this cabin?" I want to know more about his past.

Greg stands suddenly, pushing me away, his face tight with pain. "It's … not something I want to talk about, Maggie." He grips the edge of the deck, his knuckles white with tension. "You don't want to know about my past."

Chapter 15

I stand and go to him, wrapping my arms around his chest from behind. His body is tense, angry, but not with me.

"You don't have to tell me," I whisper. "But I'm here if you want to talk. No judgment. Just an old friend with as much pain in my own history. We all have scars, Greg, but perhaps we're old enough now to face the past?"

He turns around and pulls me to him, his arms holding me as an anchor against the storms of life. I've always known him to be in control, but right now, he is vulnerable. And it makes me love him more. He takes a deep breath.

"You're right, Maggie," he whispers into my hair. "Let me get some more wine." He goes back inside and brings out the bottle of Merlot, refilling our glasses as he sits back down next to me. He takes a long swig, and I wait. A cool breeze blows across the lake, bringing the scent of the forest with it.

"I was born here," Greg says finally, as he stares out across the lake. "My great-grandfather was a pioneer and started the lumber business. My father inherited this place, although he would have sold it from under us if he could have found the deeds in one of his drunken rages. Mom hid them from him, protecting the only home we had." The bitterness in his voice is still raw after so long. Perhaps the wounds from our parents never heal completely. "He beat her for that. Like he did for everything. And he beat me too, because I looked like her. My black hair and dark eyes are from her Native American ancestry."

"Did you know your grandparents on her side?"

"No. There was only Mom. She was raised in a church orphanage in Seattle after the Indian Wars, and disease wiped out thousands of Native Americans. There were no family records back then, so I could never trace her history. She trained as a household servant and, at fourteen, she was sent to a family here in McCall. She met my father at church when she was nineteen and they married, but she was never accepted. She didn't know her own people, so they were pretty much outcasts."

Greg sighs. "They had a little girl before me, my sister. I never knew her, though. She died just after I was born. Mom said she looked like him, with fair hair and blue eyes. He loved her and called her Merry Sunshine. Her name was Jenna."

I begin to understand why Greg's daughter holds such a special place in his heart. His face is strained. I gently take his hand as he continues.

"The Army draft call-up came for the war, but my father was a cripple, so he was left behind with the old guys. He drank more and more, became increasingly violent … I was away by then, studying in Austin. He beat Mom up once too often, and she had a heart attack. They arrested him, but the autopsy found she had an enlarged heart, probably genetic. So he walked free."

Greg turns his face away from me, but his voice betrays his pain.

"I didn't even know she was gone, Maggie. But Doug's mom heard from someone and got hold of me in Austin." He stares out of the window, his eyes unseeing. "I loved her so much. I only went away because she begged me to. She didn't want to see me in jail if I killed him. And I probably would have … But I went away, and he killed her."

He wipes away a tear. I squeeze his hand gently. I know the grief of losing a much-loved Mum, but not in these circumstances, and I know the guilt lies heavy on him.

"My Mom's spirit-guide was the gray wolf. She always said that I was a gray wolf like her, and that we must endure and survive. But she didn't make it."

"But you did, Greg. She would be proud of who you've become. Your business success and your family, three kids, her grandchildren, and the descendants of her people."

He smiles. "Jenna looks most like her. I wish she could have met her Grandma." His face darkens, but I can tell he wants to finish the story now. "After my father died, I hired a bulldozer and flattened the old cabin. All the rubbish of that life hauled away. I've made new memories here since then." He turns and holds me close. "I'm so glad you're here now."

The air smells of pine logs and wood smoke. The moon shines a broad swath of silver across the lake.

"How did he die?"

"Sheriff's report said he called in one afternoon in January raving about a bear in the backyard. They contacted the Rangers, but he must have gone after it with his gun."

"He shot it?"

Greg nodded. "Twice, at close range. But it went for him and near ripped his head off. Then it dragged him up there and crawled away into the forest. He was dead when the Rangers arrived. They followed the trail of blood and destroyed the bear. It was a big, old male, garbage addicted, and thin as a skeleton." He smiled, his eyes dark. "It was justice of the old kind. Gray Wolf avenged by a forest creature. My Mom's people would have been pleased. I identified the remains and it sure helped to see that sucker dead."

He takes a long sip of wine and leans back. I snuggle back under his arm. There's no real need to say anything more, and we are content in the silence together.

But under the silvery sparkle of the lake in front of us, I see dark shadows in the deep. Greg's anger at his past is so close to the surface, it could explode at any time. I've worked so hard to make my life calm and happy. Can I let him disrupt it?

* * *

Next morning, the sky is clear blue, and my bruises are healing. I feel almost human again. I head downstairs for coffee. Greg has packed a wicker picnic basket and is filling a thermos. His eyes are bright this morning as if a weight has been lifted.

"That looks interesting." I reach for the steaming coffee pot and fill a mug.

He grins. "I thought we could have breakfast out. I have a little boat. The lake is so beautiful from the water."

He bustles around getting extra layers, bundling me up in a padded coat, a scarf, hat, and gloves. "I don't want you getting cold. It's sunny out, but freezing in the wind."

We walk down to the little jetty and head out in the boat onto the water. The air hurts my lungs when I breathe, but it tastes so clean, straight off the snow-capped mountains around us. Greg stands at the wheel, back straight, his face into the sun. His smile is the same as it was when he was flying. As much as he rules the boardroom when he's in it, Greg Warren is happiest out in the expanse of nature. He really is the gray wolf, and I love to see him like this.

If only we could stay in this bubble of joy, but I feel the ticking of time passing as the sun rises higher in the sky. We both have to return to work soon, and we'll be facing each other in opposition.

And I have to go home to England, where I belong.

We head back to Boise after a light lunch, and I'm sorry to leave the cabin. But we both have to get back to work … and reality.

As we drive south again, I have to ask the question

that's been bubbling in my mind. "Have you seen anyone else since Rachel died?"

Greg shakes his head. "Barb's been trying to set me up, but I haven't been interested." He looks over and smiles. "Until now."

A warm blush spreads across my cheeks.

"Doug and I mainly talk ranch stuff, but he told me he thinks you're wonderful. That I should marry you quick."

His words catch me unawares. Did he say marry? My heart beats faster, and I laugh it off. "I bet you say that to all the girls." I lean forward and turn the radio on to stop the conversation going any further.

We drop in on Doug and Barb on the way back. The yard dogs mill around us as they greet us outside the house.

"Land sakes," Barb says when she sees my face. "That's a beauty." She gives me a gentle hug, and I'm pleased she has warmed to me.

"I'll get the kettle on," Doug says. "Or maybe a cold beer?"

"How about a little walk, Maggie?" Barb says. "Perhaps you'd like to see our place."

I nod. "I'd love to walk around the ranch."

"Look after her," Greg says, as he walks with Doug into the house.

Barb and I head for the outer barns, meandering

slowly. "Jenna told me about your fall. She's not here right now; probably for the best until those two clear the air. Father and daughter have the strength and a temper to match. Rachel used to referee, but since she's gone …"

I stop next to the corral. "Would you tell me more about her?"

Barb smiles with the warm memories of friendship. "She loved people, the church congregation, anything to do with getting folks together. She and Greg had a traditional marriage, I suppose. He was the breadwinner and head of the family. She looked after the kids, was a homemaker, and was endlessly loyal. But Greg was hard to live with at times. He can have flashes of temper and lay down the law as if he's Moses."

I nod. "I've seen him in action at work and have been on the receiving end of that temper. What happened when he retired?"

"Learning to fly channeled his restless spirit, and of course, there's always so much to do on the ranch." She sighs. "Then Rachel got sick and started to lose weight. There was nothing anyone could do."

"I know how hard that is. My Mum died of lung cancer. For two years, we did the best we could, feeling helpless, watching her suffer."

Barb nods. "Rachel had a strong faith though, and

said it was her time. But Greg never had any faith, and when she died, he was lost. After the funeral, he took off into the Payette Forest. I was worried that he might kill himself, but Doug was sure he'd come back for his children. After a few days, he returned and threw himself back into work. His hair had turned completely gray, though. It used to be jet black." Barb turns toward me. "Maggie, you're the first woman that Greg has shown any interest in since Rachel died. I haven't seen him this happy since she was well. I know she would have wanted him to find someone else."

I walk away from her and stand to look out over the land. I'm not ready to talk about my feelings for Greg with Barb. After a moment, she continues.

"She's buried on our ranch land, you know."

I turn. "Rachel's grave is here?"

"Yes, would you like to see it?"

It's a strange question, but in a way, I desperately want to see where Greg's heart is buried. Rachel is a ghost that I need to lay to rest. I nod.

"I'll tell Doug we're just going farther out and go get the truck."

Barb is back in a few minutes, and we drive in low gear up the hill to the Upper Road. There are dark woods and distant mountains across the valley. The City of Boise lies below us, and I can see the Capitol dome and even a tiny plane landing at the airport.

"The most beautiful place in the world." Barb smiles. "To my eyes, of course. The earliest French fur trappers struggled over the high desert to get here. When they saw the forest around Boise, they supposedly shouted, 'Les bois! The trees!' That's how Boise got its name. *La rivière boisée* means the wooded river."

We get out of the truck and walk through flowing grasses along a neat path. We crest the rise, and there's a simple, white headstone standing in an area of clipped grass, the grave looking out over the valley. A semi-circular stone bench sits on either side.

"Why don't you sit for a moment," Barb says. "Rachel didn't like cut flowers, so I gather wild grasses for her."

She touches the headstone gently as you might caress the arm of a dear friend and walks a little way off to pick from the tall grass. An inscription is chiseled into the stone.

Rachel Gardiner Warren. Dearly beloved wife of Greg. Adored mother of Susan, Todd, and Jenna.

I lift my eyes unto the hills, from whence cometh my salvation. Psalm 121.

It's simple and beautiful, and I feel the passing of time weigh heavily upon me. I vowed till death do us part with Duncan, but that ended in pain, not death. Greg has been through agony in losing Rachel. At this point in my life, can I risk my heart again? Can he?

Chapter 16

Barb returns with an armful of pale-blonde grass. She arranges the feathery stems in a stone vase and then sits back on her heels. She bows her head and prays silently, one hand resting on the earth. I shut my eyes, trying to pray, but nothing comes. Tears sting my eyes. This trip has been a rollercoaster, and I feel adrift from my calm life in Summerfield.

"Maggie, it's been three years since Rachel passed. She was my friend, and she would have wanted Greg to love again. I've tried to introduce him to good women in our community, but he refused to even talk to them." She smiles up at me. "Then he comes back from this last trip, and his eyes are alive again. Now you're here. I know Jenna can be a handful, but I hope you take a chance on him."

We drive slowly back to the ranch through the

rich grasslands. Back in the kitchen, Doug's sitting up at the breakfast bar alongside Greg, both munching on monster subs like happy schoolboys. The kitchen is a war zone of lettuce, cold cuts, and bread rolls.

"Fancy a sandwich?"

Barb and I giggle and join them for some food. It feels good to laugh together.

Later, Greg drives me back to the airport. "I upgraded your ticket," he says, once we're on the road. "First Class back to London. It's the least I can do."

The independent part of me instinctively wants to protest, but the cost is small change for him, and the bruises come from his horse, after all.

"Thank you." I pause for a moment. "I'm sorry I didn't get to see Jenna again. Will you tell her I said goodbye?"

Greg's hands tighten on the wheel. "I'll tell her, and I promise she'll apologize when you come back next time."

He wants me to come back. His words thrill me, but then I think of my life in England. And Jenna's anger ... and Greg's complicated life.

"Will there be a next time?" I say, softly, as we pull into the airport drop-off area. Greg parks the car and turns to me, cupping my face in his strong hands. His gray eyes are serious.

"Maggie, I want to see you again. Outside of work. In England, here, wherever."

He bends to kiss me, and I lose myself in him for those last precious moments. When we pull apart, and I am out of his arms, I feel cold, a little lost. And as he drives away, tears well up. I can't tell him yet, but this fantasy has to end here.

My generation was brought up on the first Disney films, and Cinderella was always my childhood fantasy. I knew it would be tough for a kid like me, scrubbing a lot of floors and not going to the ball. But I hoped that someday, my Prince would come.

If not the first time, then surely the second time around?

But Cinderella is a fairytale, and I can't be the evil stepmother to Greg's wayward daughter. I can't see myself by his side on the ranch when I am now longing for my English cottage in Summerfield.

My phone buzzes. A text from Greg.

Miss you already. See you in Edinburgh next week. xx

I smile and send back a smiley face and two kisses. No more than that, for now. I head into the terminal, happy to be going home.

Flying First Class is something I could definitely get used to. For the first time on a transatlantic flight,

I sleep well, on a full-length recliner with soft white sheets and a fleecy blanket. There's a limo waiting for me at Arrivals, all part of the First Class service that Greg arranged for me, and I'm grateful for it. I snooze in the back as we drive to Summerfield.

I notice that the colors of autumn are fading as we turn into the village. The leaves are dropping from the trees, and the branches are beginning to show, like skeletons against the darkening sky. The limo pulls up outside Square Cottage, and the driver helps me with my bag before driving away.

The garden is windswept and the tarpaulin flaps on the edge of the roof. A fat drop of rain lands on my face. Although I am happy to be home, my bank account is emptier now, and that dampens my residual happiness. But at least I have the next conference coming up. The money from that will fix the roof before winter sets in.

I go inside and put the kettle on. I text Greg that I'm back safely, and then I call Sam.

"Welcome home, Mum. Now spill it. I want all the details!" Her voice is excited, and I'm happy to have my daughter as a friend, rather than a constant source of conflict. I tell her about the ranch and the cabin by the lake, and she makes enthusiastic noises.

Then I pause. I have to tell her.

"What is it, Mum? Did something bad happen?"

"I had a fall. I'm still a bit bashed up, but it could have been worse."

"Oh no, that's terrible!" The sympathy in her voice makes me want to cry. So much happened in that short time away. It was an emotional rollercoaster.

"The horse I was riding rolled in a stream."

"Do you think it's time to give up riding?"

I pause for a moment, thinking of Bella and my safe, stable rides on the hills around Summerfield. "No, not at all. I'm fine riding here. I just won't be going back to Idaho. It didn't suit me too well."

"I'm sorry, Mum. But are you going to see Greg again? I can tell by your voice that you care for him."

"I'll be seeing him in Edinburgh next week at the conference. We'll see how that goes."

That night the moon is high, and the air is freezing. A potlatch night. I pull on my wooly coat and creep out to the back wall.

But the hares aren't there.

I stand looking out over the field, missing Greg's warm arms around me. How can he have disrupted my life so fast?

The week passes swiftly, and I lose myself in preparation for the conference. Greg and I text back and forth, lighthearted banter about the ranch and Summerfield. Nothing about work, although it sits between us like a giant wall, every day getting higher. How are we going to sit across from each other now?

He also sends gifts. Lots of them.

An enormous bouquet of white lilies and roses in an exquisite crystal vase is delivered by an Oxford florist. The cottage fills with the scent of summer, and I'm reminded of the exotic oriental lilies from the China Tang restaurant on our first night together.

The next day, a recording of the London Philharmonic Orchestra playing The Hebrides Overture. I put it on and close my eyes, losing myself in the majestic music, hearing echoes of laughter by a windy river in my mind. I sit on the couch in the sitting room, wrapped in a soft throw and yearning to be cuddled again in that warm overcoat.

I work in the garden every day, my thoughts often of Greg. Of what could be possible … of what might be. Daydreams of a teenager, perhaps. And I'm happy here in the life I've made for myself, so why risk it all for a dream?

But I can't stop thinking about him as I collect leaves in a big basket and carry them to enrich the compost, mulching the vegetable beds with straw. It's colder every day now, and leaves in the road chase each other in the wind. But high above the mist, the sun shines, and the sky is pale blue. I think about Greg flying the Cessna and remember the beauty of the Payette Lake and National Forest.

The next day, a carefully wrapped white box arrives, couriered from an antique shop in Oxford. I've often stood outside their window, gazing at paintings and artifacts I can't possibly afford. In the box, deep in layers of white tissue, is an exquisite pen-and-ink drawing. Two brown hares stand on their hind legs, their ears up, with sweet anxious faces, poised for flight.

Tears well up in my eyes. He might be a man of the ranch and the mountains, but Greg Warren is a romantic, and I don't know how I will face him across the boardroom and be professional about it. I just want to melt into his arms again.

Then it hits me. I should pull out of the conference. I *am* conflicted. I can't represent my client properly when I am emotionally involved with the opposition.

But the dripping from the tarpaulin reminds me that I need the money. And perhaps this has all just been a ploy to get me out of the way so that Greg can win the deal? He has always needed to win at all costs.

Doubts flood my mind.

I place the hare print behind the sofa, covering it

with a rug so it doesn't remind me of that night as I prepare to go to Edinburgh.

Chapter 17

As I board the flight to Scotland the next day, I get a text from Harry.

> I'm back in town, Mum. The photo shoot went well and finished early. Sam said you're up in Edinburgh. Can you meet for lunch today?

The conference doesn't get started until the afternoon, so I arrange to meet him for an early meal at a cafe next to the hotel. I never miss a chance to see my son, considering he's mostly gallivanting around the world as a successful photographer.

I arrive first and sit at a window table, watching for him. I can't help but smile as he rides up on his bike, waving as he locks it to a lamppost outside the cafe. I wish my Mum were alive to see him now. She loved both my children so much, but she never saw her grandson grow into the handsome man he is now. Harry looks one-hundred-percent Celt, with her red-gold hair. It seems the natural way of things that he gravitated back to Edinburgh for his university studies and now makes his home here in between traveling. His photography in fashion and dance is now appearing in national newspapers, and I'm so proud of who he's become.

Harry comes in and greets me with a monster hug, his designer stubble rasping my face. I grin from ear to ear to see him.

"Lovely to see you, Mum." I'm glad my bruises have faded now and I've covered the residual color with makeup. I wouldn't want him to worry. He sits down opposite me and then motions to the waiter. "Two rhubarb gin and tonics, please."

It's our little tradition in Edinburgh, and even though I shouldn't have one before working, I can't help but give in.

"Tell me about your trip," I say. Harry shows me photos on his phone and talks enthusiastically about his time away as we eat our light lunch. I marvel at how different we are. I've traveled so much, but he sees things I would never notice through the lens of his camera.

The door of the cafe opens, and I glance up. My heart leaps as Greg walks in. He hasn't noticed us, and he's probably just grabbing a sandwich before the conference. A blush spreads to my cheeks as I remember our time together and all the things we shared in just a few short days.

Harry sees my eyes widen and turns to look. "Who's that, Mum?"

I hold up a menu in front of my face, suddenly wishing I was someplace else. I need to compose myself before I see him again. Then Harry's face dawns with recognition. "Oh my goodness, that's Greg Warren. I remember him. He helped me get that scholarship, remember?"

I put out a hand. "Not now, Harry."

But it's too late.

Greg senses the attention and turns. His handsome face expands into a broad smile as he sees me. A smile that is most definitely not professional. He walks over. Harry stands to greet him. They shake hands as I re-introduce them.

"Good to see you again, Harry." Greg says. "I followed your progress through college. You're a photographer now, I hear."

Harry shoots an enquiring glance at me. "Yes, I am. How did you know?"

Greg looks over at me. I'm acutely aware of the faint tang of his cologne and how much I want to be in his arms. "Your Mum and I have been catching up on old times."

He bends to kiss my cheek in greeting, and as he pulls away, his hand rises to cup my face tenderly. There's no mistaking the intimate look. Harry raises an eyebrow. I turn away and look out the window.

Only to see Frances Campbell outside, a look of triumph on her face.

I inhale sharply. She saw Greg kiss me. She knows there's something going on. A chill runs down my spine. I push back my chair.

"I'm sorry, Harry. I have to go. The conference is starting soon, and I need to … get something sorted out. I'll see you inside, Greg."

I kiss my son goodbye and hurry into the conference center. I have to find Mike before Frances does. I phone him repeatedly as I run around the hotel trying to find him. I should have told him what was going on. Now it looks as if I had something to hide.

Then I see the pair of them coming out of an office near the conference center. Mike shakes Frances's hand, his face grave as he nods a goodbye. I stand still, waiting for her to leave. Then I walk up to him, trying to project confidence.

"Mike, I can explain –"

He holds up a hand. "Frances said you've been seeing Greg Warren. Is that true?"

I nod. "But we're just old friends, catching up."

"That's not what it looked like to her. She claims

that Greg's a close friend of yours and he's been consulting with you. That's a clear conflict of interest, Maggie."

"We didn't talk about work. You know me, Mike. I'm a professional, and I wouldn't jeopardize the team's work on this project."

He shakes his head. "I'm sorry, Maggie. It's because you're a professional that I'm going to have to ask you to step down and leave the project. We'll find a replacement for you. I can't have any implication of involvement that threatens our success."

He's disappointed with me, angry at having to find someone else at short notice, and I see the end of my career in his expression. Who will hire me now with allegations of improper relationships?

And I needed this job so much.

Tears well up in my eyes and I brush them away. I won't cry in front of Mike.

"I'm sorry it turned out this way, Maggie." He puts a hand on my arm. "But I need you to get all your papers and bring them to the conference room on your way out. We'll pay for your flight back, of course."

I nod and take a deep breath. At least I can leave with some dignity. "I'm sorry, too, Mike. I'll bring the papers down as soon as I get them together."

I turn away and walk back down the corridor, my

footsteps heavy as I go back to my room and gather the papers from the conference. All my preparation for nothing. My hard-won contract in flames. My career at this point unlikely to recover.

I'm no longer upset as I head back down to the conference room, but I am burning with a white-hot anger. How could I have let this happen with so much at stake?

Greg looks up as I walk in, a welcoming smile on his face. I see Mike notice the look and his face darkens. I place my papers next to Mike and shake his hand in goodbye. I turn to go.

"Maggie, aren't you staying?" Greg's voice makes me turn back. He clearly hasn't heard what happened, but from the look on Frances Campbell's face, she will be delighted to tell him that I'm off the project. I meet his gray wolf eyes and I know he sees how angry I am. I restrain my emotion and manage a measured tone.

"Goodbye, Greg."

I turn and pull the door behind me with a firm click, shutting out what I have left behind. I walk away down the corridor as tears well again in my eyes. My life was just fine before Greg Warren came back into it.

Chapter 18

I'm fuming with anger and barely notice the flight back from Edinburgh. There's a text from Greg waiting when I turn my phone back on after we land.

> I'm so sorry, Maggie. I didn't think that I would cause you so much trouble at work. Please let me make it up to you? xx

I text back and send it quickly.

> That's because you don't think of anyone but yourself. Leave me alone, Greg. You've done enough damage to my life.

He sends more texts and rings me several times that afternoon, but I ignore them all. I get back to Square Cottage and crawl into bed, defeated. My professional reputation is damaged, and at my age, it will be almost impossible to get work that pays as well.

And my heart is broken too.

I swore never to let myself be this hurt again, but I invited Greg back in. He has left me in tatters, bulldozing over my life with his dominant ways. I'm a fool, but tomorrow I'll get into the garden again. Pick yourself up, dust yourself off and start all over again, as Mum used to say. You've survived worse, Maggie Stewart.

The next morning I wake to the sound of hammering in the garden outside. I frown. That's strange. I didn't book the roofer.

I pull on a robe and look out the window. I can't quite see what's happening, but there's someone in my front garden. I hear the metallic sound of the ladder unfolding and then the bump of it leaning against the side of the cottage.

It must be a mistake. I don't have the money to pay the builder, so I need him to stop for now. I pull on my jeans and a sweater and rush downstairs. I yank open the door and step outside.

I stop, surprise rendering me speechless.

"Morning, Maggie."

Greg stands at the top of the ladder, dressed in casual jeans and a waterproof jacket. "I'm just nailing down this tarpaulin. Don't want you getting wet now."

"What the … " I'm mad at him and surprised, and under it all, my heart leaps to see him again. He's clearly left the Edinburgh conference to come after me. "Greg, what are you doing here?"

"Sorting out your roof." He looks down at me. "I may not be an expert in relationships, but I sure as hell know how to hammer nails in. I want to make sure you're warm and safe. Please, Maggie, let me do this, and then would you let me in for coffee?"

I nod. After all, the tarpaulin does need securing properly, and my independent streak doesn't stretch to the top of a ladder. "I'll put the kettle on."

Back inside, I listen to the sound of him hammering. I trust him to make it secure again, to keep out the autumn chill and I like the idea of him keeping me warm. I fill two mugs with coffee, and when he knocks on the door, I open it and invite him in. But my body language is stiff, and he doesn't try to kiss my cheek.

"I've made it secure enough to last until the builder can come." Greg takes a sip of his coffee. "Maybe I could even help him." He pauses. "I like fixing things, Maggie."

I stay standing by the sink. "Why aren't you still in Edinburgh? What happened at the conference?"

"If they don't want you, then they don't get me either." He comes to stand only inches away. "I'm so sorry, Maggie. I didn't mean to get you in trouble. I couldn't hide my feelings. When I found out what Frances did, I resigned my position and jumped on the first plane I could to get back down here." He takes my hands and I ache to be in his arms. "I've cancelled my business plans. I just want to be with you. We have so little time left and I don't want to spend it in boardrooms."

His dark eyes meet mine. "I love you, Maggie. I want to be with you." The dream of hearing him say those words has been with me forever, and joy sweeps through me. He carefully turns my face up and gently kisses my lips. "Do you think you could find a way to love me?"

I smile up at him. "I loved you from the moment we met all those years ago. But I thought you could never be mine."

"I am yours, now and forever, if you'll have me." He goes down on one knee. My heart leaps and I bite my lip, a flush rising to my cheeks. "We've been given another chance for happiness in this lifetime, and to deny this would be to deny life itself. So, would you marry me, Maggie?"

I desperately want to fall into his arms and say yes. I've dreamed of this moment. And yet, I'm petrified of what it might mean. The moment stretches on.

"I know it's a big decision," he says. "I've just sprung it on you. You don't have to say anything right now." He rises and pulls me into his arms. As he kisses me, I feel the twinge of a bruise. Can a marriage between us ever work when we are from such different worlds, living opposite lives? And then there's Jenna to consider – and my own children.

When we pull apart, I find my hands are shaking. I take a sip of my coffee. "I've pretty much given up on romantic love."

"Until now," Greg says. "Until me?"

I nod. There's so much to say, and yet, I can't bring myself to tell him.

"I'm in love with you, Maggie. I'm only truly happy when I'm near you. I love the way you laugh, the way your eyes light up when you talk about your garden and the horses. You know I have a streak of anger from my past, but I'm at peace when I'm with you."

I turn away from him, looking out into the garden. I can't do this.

"I'm sorry, Greg. I can't marry you."

Chapter 19

Greg comes to stand next to me. He puts his hand over mine. I wipe away the tears in my eyes, but I can't stop them from coming.

"What is it, Maggie? What are you scared of?"

"My first marriage wasn't like yours and Rachel's. I … I don't think I know how to be happy with someone."

Greg pulls me into his arms again. "Dear Maggie." He kisses the top of my head. "Remember that night at McCall when I told you about my painful history? It helped me so much. Please let me in."

I take a deep breath, and we sit together at the kitchen table. The robin sings from the bushes outside, an anchor to my home. I am safe here. Square Cottage is my haven. So perhaps it's time to say out loud what I have held in for so long.

"When Sam and Harry were little, I gave up my career and stayed home with them. Duncan made it very clear that he was the boss. He was always right, and never apologized. He wanted to keep me as a stay-at-home wife. When I went back to work part-time after Harry was a year old, Duncan became jealous and accused me of seeing other men. He said my job stopped me from being a good wife and mother."

Greg squeezes my hand as encouragement to continue. "Life at home was very tense. Then, when his father died, Duncan told everyone we were going back to Aberdeen. He called my boss and told him I was leaving. He went behind my back. I was so angry, but he said my only job was to have more children, to build his legacy. I felt so trapped."

I stare out at the rain, panic rising, just as it had back then.

"I couldn't bear it, Greg. We moved, and I tried, but he became mean. He bullied me, and I lost my confidence. He mocked me for putting on weight and said my hair was falling out. He was always so charming in public and so unkind at home. Never to the children, of course. He was a good dad or I'd have left much earlier, but he was cruel to me. I can see that now. He said a wife must be obedient to her husband and when I followed his rules, there was peace, but when I didn't …"

174

The past rises like a specter, the pain of those days swelling inside me. I have pushed it down for so long, and now, I can't help but let it wash over me again.

"I needed my independence. I couldn't stay, and I saw a divorce lawyer in secret. But Duncan found out and declared that there was nothing wrong with our marriage. He said that I was mentally ill, that it was all my fault, that he would fight me through every court in Scotland and I would never see my children again. I was an unfit mother and wouldn't get custody."

Tears roll down my face, like the rain on the windows. Greg pulls me into his arms.

"But you fought him?"

"Mum helped. She kept me strong, always telling me that I was a good mother, and that I could prove it. I wanted to take the children and run, but I had to do things in the proper way. I couldn't let him win." I breathe more steadily now. "I got custody every weekend, while I fought for more access. Then Duncan's mother introduced him to Fiona at a party. She was willing to be everything that I could never be, and she didn't want my kids in the way. So I got custody and Duncan had a new family. The kids love their siblings, and it's all ancient history now but ..." I turn to him, wiping my eyes with a tissue. "I'm not cut out to be a wife, Greg. I can't marry you."

He strokes my cheek. "We're not young anymore, Maggie. We both have our grown-up children, and we have both had our careers. Marriage at our age is about love and support for the next adventurous third of our lives when we get to have fun. And I'm not Duncan. Please, just think about it." He pauses and looks out at the rain. "How about we go to the stables and see Russ and Bella?"

I smile up at him. We are both at peace with horses, and it sounds like exactly the right thing to do. I'm too emotionally wrecked to talk any more. We grab coats, and I pick some apples from the fruit bowl, pushing them into my pockets.

The weather is raw outside, the rain hammering down and a chill wind blows. But as we drive over to the stables, a shaft of sunlight breaks through the clouds over the fields. It turns the gray to green again, and I can't help but smile.

We pull into the yard. Leaves whirl around us as we walk over to the stalls to see the horses. Clair's not around, and I hope Ted and May are wrapped up tight inside. They know I sometimes visit in between rides just to talk to Bella.

Bella whickers through her nose as I slip into her stall. She smells of warm hay and I stroke her silky, muscled neck. She delicately takes the crisp apple from my palm, munching happily, and I see myself reflected in her intelligent eyes.

Greg takes Russ an apple, and I hear the rumble of his voice in the stall next door, as the rain beats down on the tin roof. I feel at peace and I wonder if marriage to Greg could possibly be as good as this.

Later that evening, we sit together in the warmth of the cottage as a storm howls outside. Greg goes out to check that the tarpaulin will hold and then comes back in, dripping wet but with a wide grin on his face.

"That's a good job, if I do say so myself." He holds up a bottle. "I also got this from the car."

He takes off his raincoat and then grabs a corkscrew and opens the bottle to let it breathe. "Chateau Lafitte Rothschild. Bordeaux Pauillac. Described as intense, subtle and complex." He grins. "I thought of you."

"I don't know anything about fine wines."

He smiles. "Perhaps we both have a lot to learn."

He fetches two of my best glasses and polishes them, holding them up to the light to check the clarity. He carefully pours me a glass and then raises his own to his nose. He breathes in the bouquet, and I smile to see the pleasure on his face. I take a sip, and the wine has layers of color, like a painting in my mouth.

"What do you think?" Greg asks.

I pause, savoring the aftertaste. "Autumn tones of plum, honey and a hint of turmeric?"

"Pretty good!" We laugh together, and he pulls me close. We sit watching the flames, enjoying our wine.

"Have you thought any more about what I asked you?" Greg's voice is tentative, careful.

I sigh a little. "I feel bad about bringing up that ancient history."

Greg's eyes are tender. "I'm so glad you told me, and besides, think of all the awful stuff I confessed in McCall. Your marriage to Duncan was not an equal partnership. Marriage should be more like a wolf pack, with an alpha female as well as an alpha male. They're both leaders." He squeezes my hand. "We can be married like that: different, but equal."

"Please, just give me a little time to think about it."

Greg stares into the fire for a moment. "We're not so young anymore, Maggie. How much time do we have left to be happy?"

Chapter 20

The next morning, Greg comes down and wraps me in a bear hug. I relish his warmth and lean into him. It feels so good to be his arms. How could I want to be anywhere else, and yet ...

"How did you sleep?" His eyes betray a deeper question.

"I've been thinking a lot, and I'd love you to meet my daughter, Sam, and her husband, Luke. I trust Sam's judgment."

"So if she likes me, I might have a chance?" Greg raises an eyebrow.

I nod. "I guess so. At least it might help me get some perspective."

"Before we go anywhere, we need pancakes."

"Good idea. Pancakes would be great."

He squeezes orange juice while I mix the batter,

pour and flip. Then we take everything into the garden room on trays. Greg pours maple syrup onto his stack of pancakes and slices a banana on the top.

"Todd taught me how to make pancakes," he says quietly. "You're such good friends with your children. I think it's time I made more of an effort with my own."

I'm thrilled to hear him talk about a different kind of future, one where conflict doesn't become his default position.

After breakfast, we drive to Sam and Luke's place on the outskirts of Oxford.

"Anything I should know before we get there?" Greg's usually confident voice is just a little tentative, and I smile inwardly, glad that he cares enough to be concerned about what my daughter might think of him.

"Sam's lovely, Greg. She writes thriller novels but also works at the Oxford University Press a few days a week where she helps edit academic books. Luke has a lecturer and researcher position in biochemistry."

"Any kids?"

"Not yet. Maybe not ever. They have a lot going on."

Greg looks over and takes my hand. "Things are

different than when we were young, that's for sure. I'm looking forward to meeting them."

We park, and Greg pulls a bottle of vintage champagne from the back seat. I'm touched that he wanted to bring something so classy when I usually turn up with a half-decent merlot. Sam must have heard the car because she pulls open the door and rushes out. Her blonde hair is tied back from her face and her blue eyes sparkle as she sees us. I notice her eyebrows arch a little as she looks at Greg and smiles conspiratorially at me. I'm secretly pleased that my daughter thinks he's good looking.

"Hi, Mum!" She leans in and kisses my cheek and then turns. "And you must be Greg. I've heard a lot about you."

Greg puts out a hand, and Sam shakes it and then leans in for a friendly kiss. She's much more European than I am, and people in publishing seem to be a lot more 'touchy-feely.' Greg gives her the champagne.

"Oh, thank you. I'll put this to chill before lunch. Come inside. The roast's almost ready."

We walk inside, and the succulent smell of roasting meat fills the air. Luke stands in the hallway, his sandy hair bleached a little by last summer's sun. He coaches one of the St. Peter's College rowing eights, so he spends months cycling up and down the towpath.

No sooner do I introduce Greg than Luke grabs two beers, and they sit down at his computer to look at some biochemical modeling for a new project. Greg knows quite a bit about biochemistry from the oil company, and he gets Luke talking. Sam and I head into the kitchen.

"Didn't take them long to get acquainted, did it?" Samantha says, laughing. I sit up at her countertop with a gin and tonic, as she prepares green beans, topping and tailing them into a colander. She turns to whisper. "Greg's pretty hot, Mum."

I giggle and then pause a little too long. She notices. "What is it?"

"He asked me to marry him."

Sam leaves the beans and wraps her arms around me, squeezing tight. "I'm so thrilled for you. He seems like a great guy, and when you talk about him, you glow." Then she pulls away, sensing my concern. "What's wrong? Don't you want to be with him?"

I take a sip of my gin and tonic, needing the moment. "I want to, so much. But I'm terrified that it will be like the ocean cruise I went on. I looked forward to it and was so convinced it was what I wanted. But in the end I was desperately claustrophobic, with no ability to get off." I sigh. "Your Dad and I struggled, you know that, but I see you and

Luke as happily married partners. I just don't know whether it's possible for me now."

Sam resumes preparing the vegetables, cutting a cauliflower into florets and putting them on to steam. "Oh Mum, nothing's ever perfect. Luke and I have to work on the balance all the time. Of course, there will be hard times, but it's absolutely worth it."

"Perhaps I've been on my own too long to start again."

"But would you be happier with him than without him?" She takes my hand. "You know I just want you to be happy, Mum. You have a great life, but sometimes I worry that you're lonely."

Of course, she's right. As much as I value my independence, there are times when all I want is someone to talk with, someone to hold onto when the storms rage outside, someone to love and who loves me. Sam continues.

"It's lovely to see you two together, holding hands when you think no one is watching, as if you belong together. He makes you laugh, and you seem happier, Mum."

But my mind is wracked with doubts. "There has to be a flaw I can't see."

"Of course, there will always be flaws, in both of you. Are you trying to find flaws, Mum? Do you think you're so perfect?" She says this with a smile, but I know she means it, too.

"He has baggage."

"You're carrying baggage, too, Mum. Perhaps more than you know. Your marriage to Dad was a generation ago now. You were so young when you were together. You didn't know yourselves. It's a different time now, and you and Greg can truly be equals."

I gulp at the gin and tonic and the bitter taste helps anchor me. "I'm so confused as to what I really want."

"Making a big change like this is scary. Sharing your life with someone else is a risk, and I felt the same when Luke and I got married. We've both had to be open to change to make it work." The oven pings. "Right, the roast is done."

Sam grabs padded gloves and pulls a huge tray of roast beef out of the oven. It smells delicious. She sets it to rest and turns back to me.

"Remember that you get to choose, Mum. You don't need a man, that's clear, but do you want this one? It will be a challenge, but you've never shied away from that. What do you want for the next third of your life?"

Together, we transfer the vegetables into covered dishes. Sam checks everything.

"Roast potatoes, parsnips, carrots, braised red cabbage, cauliflower cheese. Plus homemade

Yorkshire puddings, mustard and plenty of gravy."

"This is amazing, Sam."

"I wanted it to be special, Mum. I want Greg to feel welcome in our family." She finishes the gravy, and we take everything into the living room.

Luke opens the champagne. "What shall we toast?" he asks, as he pours us all a glass.

"New beginnings," I say, quietly. Greg smiles and takes my hand under the table.

"New beginnings," we all say together.

Luke carves the roast and Sam serves us all a huge plate of wonderful food. She brings the gravy in from the kitchen, the scent of herbs wafting in the air. It feels like a celebration!

"Remember that antiques market where we bought this gravy jug, Mum?" She laughs. "Crazy place. We ended up getting lost in a maze of old French shutters, vintage bath tubs, and china knick-knacks." She looks over at Greg. "Mum gets really cranky when she gets lost." She grins.

Oh no, it looks like payback for all the times I've embarrassed her with little stories from the past. But I don't need to worry. My daughter only wants the best for me.

"Remember that time we rode in the New Forest? A whole lot of wild pigs were snuffling about in the leaves and the sun was shining through the dappled trees. It's a shame we don't get to ride much together anymore."

"Do you ride, Luke?" Greg asks.

"Not really," Luke takes a sip of the champagne. "But Sam and I had a lovely ride in New Zealand in a place called Paradise that looked pristine, as if no human had ever been there."

Greg asks lots of questions about their trip to New Zealand, so Luke and Sam talk enthusiastically about the North and South Islands. I've heard them talk about it before, and I definitely want to go some day.

"You need a couple of months, or more, if you can." Luke piles his plate with a second helping of vegetables. He pours a lake of fragrant, meaty gravy onto his plate. "There's so much to see and do." He turns to Sam and touches her hand. "It's a special place for us."

Sam smiles. "Yes, and we want to go again to walk the Milford Track. You guys should go."

Conversation flows easily around travel and work projects, families and experiences. The wine stops me from analyzing, and I enjoy just being in the moment.

"Roast dinner on Sundays is always a treat." Luke gives a sigh of satisfaction and pats his slightly rounded tummy. "Thank you, amazing wife."

"It's great that you have such a traditional marriage," Greg says, and I realize that he's taken Luke's comment out of context. But he doesn't stop. "Women are much better in the kitchen, and it seems like your work is important, Luke. I imagine you're so busy, it must be wonderful to have Sam help at home."

Sam's face has a look I know well. An expression reserved for old men who don't take her work seriously, who underestimate her role. There are enough of those in Oxford that she recognizes them a mile off. Now Greg has assumed that mantle, and I see my daughter's anger rise. Luke tries to head off an argument.

"Our marriage isn't so traditional, actually. Sam earns more than I do, and I cook during the week when Sam often works later."

Greg's eyes widen. "Really, that's so surprising."

"Seriously?" Sam can't help herself. "What kind of workplace do you have in your company, Greg, if you don't think a woman can be equal to, or even better than, a man?"

Greg launches into a defense of his company policies and the tension rises. Sam crosses her arms, her eyebrows furrowed and Luke takes a swig of wine as if settling in for the long haul. He doesn't shy from an argument, but I can't cope with this conflict, not with my family. How dare Greg bring his opinions here and fight with those I love?

I push back my chair and rush out into the kitchen, my breath hitching in a barely contained sob.

Chapter 21

Sam comes after me.

"Mum?" I turn and sob onto her shoulder. She hugs me and pats my back. "I'm sorry. I just –"

"Maggie?" Greg's voice from the doorway is contrite. I turn my face away from him and wipe my eyes as he continues. "I'm so sorry, I … I guess I said the wrong thing." He takes a step into the kitchen. "Sam, I apologize. I wouldn't dream of disrespecting you or your life here. I'm from a different generation, but I want you to know that I have amazing daughters and granddaughters. I want the very best for them, and you are a wonderful example. Please forgive me?"

I sniff a little and pull back from Sam. I want to see her face. I want to see how she reacts to Greg, and I'm so relieved to see her smile.

"Don't worry at all." Sam steps forward and embraces Greg. "This family will soon buff your corners off. Mum won't let you get away with it."

Greg turns to me. "Maggie, I'm sorry you're upset. Please, give me another chance?"

The oven pings again.

"Maybe we can try again over cinnamon and apple crumble?" Sam opens the oven door and now the room smells of sweet fruit and spices. Luke comes to the doorway. "With custard, cream or vanilla ice cream?" he asks. "Or all of them, like I'm having."

They're all looking at me. I grab a piece of kitchen towel and blow my nose. Sam giggles at the noise, and I can't help but smile.

"I'll have a huge piece." I take Greg's hand, and we walk back into the living room. "And then I'll beat you all at Scrabble."

* * *

As we drive back to Square Cottage later that evening, I'm happy that we managed to make it through the rest of the afternoon without conflict. Maybe it's naive of me to think life will pass so smoothly, but it was like a first family date.

The sky grows dark, and the headlights catch the hedgerows as we near Summerfield.

"They're a great couple," Greg says. "You must be very proud. I only hope Jenna can find someone who respects her like Luke does Sam."

I pull into the garage and turn off the engine. "There's someone for everyone," I whisper. "And perhaps sometimes there's more than one person in a lifetime. Is it too late for us?"

He leans forward and cups the back of my neck, pulling my face to his. "It's only too late if you say no to this chance, Maggie." He bends to kiss me gently on the lips. A sweet kiss that's tender with love. A kiss that shows respect for the woman I am now, and for the past we both have. He pulls away. "Now let's go inside and get the fire on. I'm going to put your apron on tonight and cook you dinner."

I groan. "I'm still stuffed from lunch. I can't think about dinner."

"Doesn't matter." Greg unfolds himself from the car. "I have to prove I respect you as an independent woman." I bat his arm as we giggle together and go into the cottage.

Greg lights the fire, posing in a manly way with the logs, making me laugh even more. It feels good to laugh. And it's then I realize what I've been missing.

He brings joy into my life. He adds to the life I have built for myself. I don't need to think about what I might lose by marrying him, but only what we might be together. The flicker of the flames lights his face as he concentrates on fanning it into life. My heart is like that tiny spark and only he can make it warm and glowing again.

He turns, aware of my eyes on him. "What is it?" He comes closer, and I can smell the wood smoke on him, the scent of my home on his skin.

"I …" I look up at him and bite my lip. My heart is hammering. "You know what you asked me before? Well, maybe you could –"

His eyes light up. "You mean I could ask you again?"

I nod my head. He gets up quickly. "Just a minute!"

He sprints upstairs, his footsteps pounding the floorboards. He returns quickly with a small, blue, velvet box. He drops to one knee on the rug, the firelight illuminating his sincere face, and places the box next to him.

He takes my hands in his, his eyes shining with love. "Maggie, I love you. I want you to be my wife and spend the rest of our lives together. Please, will you marry me?"

"Dearest Greg." I lean forward so he can see I've made it through the anxiety and really mean what I'm saying. "Yes, please, with all my heart. I love you and want to be your wife. I will marry you."

He squeezes my hands and bends to kiss me sweetly. Then pulls away. "I hope you like this." He opens the tiny blue box. An antique engagement ring glows on a bed of white satin. An oval sapphire surrounded by diamonds and set in pale gold.

"It's your birthstone and the gold is quite rare, from the Hebrides Islands, so you'll always have a piece of Scotland. But we can find another one if you don't like it."

I stroke the ring with the tip of one finger. "It's stunning. I love it."

He takes the ring from the box. "It may not be exactly right, but I sized your ring finger against my little one when we were holding hands in the limo. May I see if it fits?"

I nod, trembling a little. With relief, joy, and anticipation, tears sting my eyes, and I wipe one away as Greg slips the gorgeous ring onto the engagement finger of my left hand.

He kisses my hand and then kisses away the tears of happiness from my cheeks. "You're really sure?"

"Yes." I touch the ring. It feels heavy on my hand but I know I'll get used to the change. "I'm really sure this time. I know it won't all be roses, but we'll muddle through together. There have been opportunities in my life that I didn't take, but you're right, we need to make the most of the time we have left. I want to spend my time with you."

He goes back into the kitchen to get the half-bottle of Chateau Lafitte and pours us a glass. There will be more than enough champagne to come, and this feels right now. Greg raises his glass. "To us and the future, Maggie."

"And to you, my persistent love."

* * *

Two weeks later, I'm standing in my bedroom looking out across the green hills on the outskirts of Summerfield. Horses canter across the top of the field, as wild as the wind that whips the branches outside my window. I'm surrounded by boxes and packing materials, and I'm waiting for Sam to arrive. I need her help today.

Once we made the decision, my life has spun into a whirlwind of organization as we try to sort out the details of the wedding. After all, why wait any longer? We've already spent enough time apart.

Greg has been true to his word and rearranged his work commitments. He's up in London today sorting out some final details, and after so long in charge, he's taking a step back. We'll be able to travel, to see the places we've always wanted to go, but together this time. We've booked a few months in New Zealand after the wedding, and I'm excited to go there with him, to see the world through a new pair of eyes, as Mrs. Warren. The name feels strange on my tongue, but it will become more comfortable with time, like a new pair of riding boots.

I hear Sam's car in the drive, the slam of her door and her footsteps on the path.

"Mum?" She calls as she enters.

"Up here."

Sam comes into my room brandishing a bag from Lizzie's bakery stall in the village. "Fresh baked chocolate brownies. Fuel for packing!"

We hug, and she goes back down to make tea, while I sit in the chaos. It's hard for me to leave Square Cottage, but I'm ready to start the next phase of my life. After all, we'll come back here every summer. We'll split our time between America and England and when we're this side of 'the pond,' we'll stay at Summerfield.

But I want our family and friends to be able to enjoy it when we're away, plus the place needs warmth and love. I don't like to leave it empty for long, especially when the garden needs looking after. Thankfully, Selena from the Potlatch Inn will manage it for me when I'm not here, and I couldn't think of a better person.

But first, I need to make the cottage shipshape, so it will be ready for visitors, so I'm boxing all of my personal stuff up. I look up at the old wooden beams and smile. This house has had a lot of love in it, and I know there's much more to come, for Greg and me, and for our family.

Sam comes back up with the tea. "Right, let's get this stuff sorted." She reaches into a box, pulls out a long ruddy orange scarf and grimaces. "I hope this is going to charity?"

I laugh. "I'm taking the opportunity to have a good clear out. I haven't worn that since around 1986."

"Ooh, have you got some of those shoulder-padded business suits you used to wear back then? Those were priceless."

We giggle together, reminiscing about old times as we pack up the boxes. Some for the charity shop, some for the dump. My personal things will be wrapped in tissue paper and kept here. I'll lock up my bedroom so people can use the other rooms, but this will remain my sanctuary.

Sam sprays furniture polish and wipes the dust from the back of my old chest. "So, you're back in Boise for Thanksgiving next week?"

I nod. "I still haven't even talked to Jenna since I was over there. We need to clear the air about the wedding." My pulse accelerates to even think of that potential conflict, but I desperately want to make things right before the big day. Greg's face clouds every time he speaks to her, and it's clear everything is not okay, but I can only hope we'll do better in person.

Sam puts her hand on my arm. "It'll be okay, Mum. She'll come around."

I sigh. "I hope so. I just want our family to be happy."

"Oh, look at this." Sam pulls out an old photo album, and we sit on the floor together and look at the pages. The pictures are faded, stuck on with glue, edges peeling up. Little Harry plays in a paddling pool in the garden, sun on his face, while Sam paints, her face concentrating on her brush. I put my arm around my daughter and pull her close for a hug.

"I have so many happy memories of you and Harry growing up here."

Sam smiles. "You did an amazing job, Mum. I know things were hard at times, but you gave us a fantastic life. And I'm glad you're not going to sell Square Cottage. It's a special place."

I look around and smile. "Yes, it is." Even though I'm starting again with Greg, it's comforting to know that I can always come back here. Square Cottage in Summerfield will always be a place of refuge, but my new home is with my husband, wherever we choose to roam.

Chapter 22

As I step onto the plane this time, my hand is in Greg's, and we turn into First Class, a world away from that flight to Edinburgh, the morning we met again. How my life has changed, and all for the better.

We sit in luxurious seats next to each other, glasses of champagne in hand and look over all the details for our trip. Half the fun is anticipation, and once you're in the air, there's nothing to do until landing, so we relax and dream.

"I'm looking forward to whale watching in Kaikoura." Greg scrolls down the list from the personal travel agent on his laptop. "And the TranzAlpine train. Wine tours and vineyards in Napier and Gisborne."

I lean over to look at the pictures on his screen.

"Bubbling mud pools in Rotorua. Sam says it's like Yellowstone but wilder, with no guard rails or restrooms. Enter at your peril." I pause, noting the details of our hotel accommodation. "Although that sounds like an exclusive spa." I can't help but smile. Money isn't an issue anymore. No more leaky roofs and cold attic garrets. My independent streak is happy to still have Square Cottage in my sole name, but Greg is so thrilled to share his good fortune, and I'm starting to enjoy this new reality.

We have a delicious meal from the *a la carte* menu and afterwards, while we're sipping green tea, Greg pulls up the Tiffany catalog on his phone. He scrolls through pages of stunning jewelry, before stopping at the sapphires.

"I know we've chosen plain wedding bands, but I want to get you something beautiful to match your engagement ring. You said your dress is a soft blue. May I buy you a necklace and earrings to go with it, to commemorate our happy day?"

The precious stones are all from Sri Lanka, the sapphire capital of the world. The old Maggie would have protested her independence. But I now see the pleasure Greg gets from giving, so we have fun together looking at gemstones and eventually choose a dazzling sapphire necklace with matching pendant earrings.

"Thank you. I love them." I kiss him softly.

"I'll keep buying you presents if you keep kissing me," he murmurs. We giggle together, suddenly aware of those around us. He pulls away. "It's traditional for the groom to thank the bridesmaids with gifts." He turns back to the brochure. "What about these for Sky and Shelby?" He shows me rose-pink sapphire pendants, smaller and pretty for young girls.

"They're beautiful."

The flight passes quickly, and we arrive in Boise, via Seattle, on the evening before Thanksgiving.

Barb meets us at the airport. She hugs me, and I know she will be a true friend.

"Any news from Jenna?" Greg's face is a mask of concern. "Is she coming tomorrow?"

Barb shakes her head. "Sorry, she's still not speaking to us, either. I think she's staying in Seattle with her aunt again." She grips Greg's hand. "She'll come around, don't you worry."

But her words sound hollow, and I can only hope that Jenna's anger softens before the wedding.

Barb drops us at a new luxury apartment complex in town and indicates Greg's truck under the shelter. "Doug brought it down for you. The keys are inside. I have to run, but I'll see you tomorrow afternoon for the Thanksgiving barbecue."

"Can we come and help you in the morning?"

"Thanks, Maggie, but we've got helpers-a-plenty. It's your first Thanksgiving together with us, so we want you to come as guests. See you tomorrow."

The jet lag hits and we both head for bed.

I fall asleep quickly but wake before dawn with the jet lag. It feels strange for a moment, the sheets too crisp, the air too sharp. But then I know Greg is next door, and that it won't be long until we are together. I can't help but smile in anticipation.

There's only one shadow on our happiness – Jenna. Will she come for Thanksgiving? I can only hope that she will soften and join us on a day meant for family.

Greg and I have a restful morning, walking along the Boise River Greenbelt path through the heart of the city under the spreading cottonwood trees. Later, we drive to Doug and Barb's, parking behind the barn with all the other trucks, and I realize that this is more of a community event than I had anticipated.

"You ready?" Greg says, turning to me before we get out. "I haven't brought a woman to anything since Rachel, so I know people will be interested in you." He kisses my hand with the engagement ring on it.

I take a deep breath. "Ready."

The yard in front of the ranch house is strung with colorful bunting, and there are big tables heaped full of food. All the local families are here today and the buzz of talking and laughter fills the air. Doug is carving, his face all smiles as he greets everyone by name. Thanksgiving is for celebrating the bounteous harvest, for appreciating family and friends, and everyone gets to eat D-Bar beef today. Kids run around with excited squeals, chasing each other and having fun.

Greg navigates the crowd, introducing me as his fiancée, and I blush a little under the heat of his gaze and the pride in his voice.

The sun sets and hundreds of twinkling lights switch on. We drift quietly into the shadows and lean on the fence, looking up at the gathering dark of the National Forest. A flock of Canada geese fly overhead on their migration route, calling to one another on the wind. They live between two places, happily traveling every year, so perhaps we will be like them.

"Are you enjoying Thanksgiving?" Greg asks. "I know it can be a little intense."

"It's lovely to see you here with family and friends, and to know I will be by your side in years to come."

He leans down and kisses me. But I sense sadness behind his smile, and I know it's because of Jenna.

She's never missed a Thanksgiving before. I pull away and take his hand.

"You need to go see her," I whisper. "It doesn't matter anymore who said or did what. We need our whole family at our wedding."

He nods. "We'll make it right."

Country music starts up behind us, and I turn to see three fiddlers step onto the small stage as people throng the dancing area. We applaud as Doug and Barb take to the floor and lead a two-step as others join them.

"Get over here, you two!" Barb calls over.

Greg takes my hand. "You might as well start learning." He laughs and pulls me onto the dance floor.

Much later, after a fun evening of dancing and laughter, we head toward the truck. The moon is high, and families wrap sleepy children in blankets, packing them into trucks with empty food baskets in the back. Another year passes, and we are all grateful for one another.

"Goodnight." I wave to Barb and Doug. "Thank you for a great first Thanksgiving. See you tomorrow."

The strings of party lights go out as we follow the other trucks along the Lower Road. A gray wolf howls from high above us in the forest, and I wonder whether the pack watches us from under the trees. Greg takes my hand, and we drive back to the apartment.

The morning after Thanksgiving I'm the first one up. I look out the window and call for Greg with excitement.

"The foothills have snow! It's like icing sugar on a Christmas pudding."

Greg comes and stands next to me at the big window, arm around my shoulders, and we look up at the hills and the tops of the distant mountains beyond.

"I love seeing my world again through your eyes," he says. "It makes it all fresh and new."

He makes coffee, toast and a fruit plate and sets it on the table overlooking the stunning view. He still hasn't mentioned Jenna.

"Tell me about Black Friday." I munch my toast. "I've only seen the advertising about bargains at the mall, so what's the parade about today?"

"It's the Native American Heritage Day, set up by Congress to pay tribute to Native Americans for their contributions to the United States. But it's also a day of mourning when we commemorate the ancestors who died in the Indian Wars and afterwards. Riderless horses are led silently in the parade, and everyone wears their tribal regalia.

I go every year to honor my Mom, and this year three of Barb's rescue Appaloosas are taking part." He frowns. "Jenna usually goes with us. She hasn't missed a year."

His voice trails off, and he grabs his mobile phone. He dials, then waits and waits. His face falls as the line goes to voicemail and he puts the phone down again.

We meet Barb and Doug at the fairgrounds later. We walk through the crowds, Greg and Doug striding in front, and I stroll along with Barb behind.

"I heard from Todd last night," she says. "He said he's coming to the wedding." She puts a hand on my arm. "He wants to try and mend things with his Dad. This is a great chance for the family to come together, Maggie. We haven't seen Todd since the funeral, and he reminds me so much of Rachel."

"Is that why Greg finds it difficult to be with him?"

Barb shakes her head. "Greg had a fixed idea of what an Idaho man should do. But Todd never took to riding or the ranch, like Jenna did. He loved to cook and ended up at a Cordon Bleu College in Paris and became a chef in Europe."

"I'm looking forward to meeting him. Is there any news from Jenna?"

Barb shakes her head. "I'm worried. She's never

missed a Black Friday Parade. Blue came down from the Upper Road early this morning, but there's no sign of her yet."

We stand with Greg and Doug, their baseball caps off, as the parade passes. All the horses, many of them Appaloosas, are wearing beautifully decorated halters and saddle blankets.

My hand is in Greg's and suddenly, I feel him tense. His grip tightens. I look up at his face. He's staring at the horizon.

Jenna stands next to Blue on top of the opposite hill, silhouetted against the sky, the Spirit Horse of an ancient people. Her hair is in two long dark braids, and she's wearing traditional costume.

As the Black Friday Parade passes with muffled hooves, she stays motionless, looking down at the riders with respect. After they walk by, Jenna jumps up on Blue. They wheel away and gallop over the crest of the hill, away from us.

Greg turns to me. "I need to go after her, Maggie." His eyes are desperately worried. "What if she doesn't come back this time?"

Doug nudges him. "Wait, Greg. Look over there."

We turn to the bottom of the hill to see Jenna holding Blue's halter, walking slowly through the crowd toward us. People take pictures of them, slowing their progress, but she fixes her eyes on her Dad. Greg stands in silence, waiting for her.

She finally reaches us and Blue stands at rest. He nuzzles against me.

Jenna smiles. "He has good judgment about people." She pauses and takes a deep breath. "I'm sorry, Maggie. For what happened that day in the stream, for being angry and leaving. I didn't mean for you to get hurt. Please forgive me."

I can see in her eyes that she means it. "Of course, Jenna. I'm sorry too." I open my arms, and she hugs me. Then she turns to Greg.

"I'm sorry for being a pain, Dad. Can I come to the wedding?"

Greg grins and pulls his daughter close. "Only if you dance with me."

We laugh together. My worries fall away. Now we can be married with all our family around us.

Chapter 23

The wedding day dawns bright and clear. I wake suddenly and bolt upright. Is it really today? Am I actually doing this?

I pull on a robe and pad out onto the deck of the bridal suite. The sunshine sparkles on the water and the breeze brings the scent of bougainvillea. As much as I love Summerfield, it's cold and wet in the winter, and I'm glad we decided to marry here in the sun at La Jolla Shores in San Diego. This is where we first connected all those years ago, and it feels right to come full circle back here, when so much has changed.

I wish Greg were here with me now, but I won't see him until I walk down the aisle. My heart flutters. It really is today.

There's a knock at the door. "Mum, it's me." Sam's

soft voice is calling me, and I smile. I'm glad she's here.

I open the door. She stands there with coffee in paper cups and a bag that smells like pastries.

"I knew you'd be up." She grins and waves the bag as she comes in." Jet-lag hungry and nervous?"

"You know me so well."

We eat on the deck and relax with our coffee. There's no rush, and I am content to be here with her in a moment of stillness. Then she points with excitement.

"Look down there!" A sea lion swims along the curl of a turquoise wave. Happiness curls inside me as it delights in the morning water. Life goes on. Greg and I will have our moments of conflict, like any couple, but we will make it.

The spa is booked for all the preparations, so Sam and I go down to meet the others. While the men are out golfing, the women head for some luxury and, for once in my life, professional hair and makeup.

Manicures, pedicures and treatments in the spa. Chattering, giggling and shrieks, and interesting conversations with women we've just met, or haven't seen for a long time.

When we return to the bridal suite for lunch, there are pitchers of ice-cold peach tea, baskets of tiny pastries, heaping platters of delicate sandwiches, and salads lightly covered with white linen napkins. Sky and Shelby keep returning to the strawberries dipped in chocolate, until Susan spots them and tells them that if they have any more, they'll be sick.

The hair stylist piles some of my hair on top of my head and uses a curling iron to make long, loose curls at one side. The makeup artist does a magical job. Natural makeup, but just enough so I look like a more glamorous version of me.

"You look fantastic, Maggie." Barb pats me on the arm. "Greg is a lucky man."

Skylar and Shelby now have their silky hair curled into long ringlets, held in place with tiny circlets of flowers. Sam takes them over to a couch to read favorite storybooks. It's getting closer to the time when I will see Greg in the aisle, and my stomach does little flips as I think about him waiting for me.

Sam and I go back into the bedroom, and she helps me put my dress on. We giggle together, like two little girls playing dress-up before the performance of a play. The sky blue silk whispers over my body, like it weighs nothing at all. I put on the sapphire earrings and necklace that Greg bought for me, and Sam helps me with the fascinator with the subtle veil.

Not quite the young blushing bride, but my eyes are shining with happiness. This Maggie Stewart is quite different from the one who flew to Edinburgh that morning and met Greg on the plane.

I take a deep breath. Sam smiles at me in the mirror. "It's going to be fine, Mum. You deserve to be happy." She grabs a tissue. "No tears now. You'll ruin your makeup."

We go back into the sitting room, and I twirl around.

"You look beautiful," Susan says, with a kind smile for me.

"Like a princess," Shelby whispers as she touches the skirt of my dress with gentle fingers.

"And you are a pretty pair of flower girls." I bend and give Skylar and Shelby a cuddle. In their floral dresses, with the pink sapphire necklaces from their Pops, they look perfect.

There's a knock at the door.

"It's almost time, Mum. Are you ready?" Harry walks in wearing a dress kilt in Hunting Stewart tartan with a black Prince Charlie jacket on top. Underneath, he wears a frilled white shirt with a black string tie and black waistcoat. Cream knee socks, dress brogues, a black and silver sporran on a silver chain, and an ornamental dagger in the top of his right stocking complete the outfit. I wish Mum were here to see him representing her Scottish heritage in America.

He bends to kiss me. "You look lovely."

Sam hands me the delicate bridal bouquet, fragrant white lilies nestling in lacy green foliage.

"Nan would have loved to see you so happy," Harry says, and I nearly cry again.

"You don't think I'm too old to be doing this?"

"Not at all," Sam says. Harry shakes his head and laughs, and the three of us have a hug. My two wonderful children here with me at the start of another great adventure.

Harry turns me to face the long mirror, and I gaze at the two people reflected there. I look younger and slimmer, smiling and holding the arm of a red-haired man in Highland dress. The floor-length, blue and silver gown shimmers softly, and my upswept hair gives me height. Gleaming corn-colored wisps soften my face, and the matching fascinator is tilted, the tiny net saucily covering my left eye and part of one cheek.

Star sapphire earrings match an exquisite sapphire necklace, lying in the neckline of the beautiful wedding dress. Greg's exquisite engagement ring sparkles on my left hand. I take a deep breath and give a sigh of contentment. Today I'm marrying the man I love.

Susan and the girls lead the way to the top of the sweeping staircase, and I hear flutes playing a lilting

Mozart piece downstairs. I imagine the guests all waiting for me with excitement.

Skylar and Shelby walk carefully down the stairs, scattering rose petals along the short hallway leading to the beautiful LaJolla Room where the wedding will take place. It reminds me of the potpourri I use at Square Cottage, and I think of the scent of summer lingering back in Summerfield.

I've come a long way to be here.

Leaning on Harry's arm, I walk down the stairs. We pause at the door, and the music changes. The two flower girls enter, followed by our three beautiful daughters, Sam, Susan, and Jenna. Greg and I are so lucky to have had lives before each other, and now our adventure begins anew.

Harry turns to me. "Ready, Mum?"

I nod, unable to speak.

We walk into the room, and Harry guides me slowly down the central aisle. The rustle of silk fans out behind me and, as if from far away, I see Greg. He stands tall, almost regal, and his gray wolf eyes are fixed on me, full of love.

Greg Warren is waiting to marry me.

It seems like a dream, but here we are. We made it.

I blush a little under his gaze as we walk the short distance to his side.

"Be happy, Mum," Harry whispers before moving away.

Greg reaches for my hand and squeezes it. I want him to pull me into his arms. "You look beautiful," he mouths at me, and I feel like a teenager again, buoyed up by his love and the happy faces of those we love around us. The celebrant begins.

"Welcome, everyone, to Greg and Maggie's wedding. Barbara will begin our ceremony with a reading."

Barb stands and smiles at us both.

"If I speak in the tongues of men or of angels, but do not have love, I am a resounding gong or a clanging cymbal …"

As she reads, I let the words wash over me. "… So remain these three: faith, hope, and love. And the greatest of these is love."

Todd comes forward with our gold wedding rings on a small Celtic pillow. He nods to his father and smiles at me. It's so special to have all our children here around us.

"We are gathered here today to witness Maggie and Greg's vows of matrimony and partnership." He gestures to us both, and we turn to face each other.

Greg takes my left hand in his. He looks into my eyes, and I see happy tears sparkling there.

"Maggie. After a long time apart, we met again, and you turned my darkness into light. Today, I declare my love for you." Greg places the wedding band upon my finger, carefully fitting it against the sapphire engagement ring.

I take his ring from the velvet cushion and hold it tightly in my right hand, looking up into his eyes. "Greg, I loved you from the first moment we met, but our partnership was not meant to be. Until today. I'm filled with joy when I think of spending the rest of our lives together." I carefully slide the wedding ring onto his finger and hold his hand in both of mine. We face each other as if no one else exists.

"Maggie, I promise to love you, to honor and respect you. To cherish you and look after you, until death parts us. On this wonderful day, with our dear ones around us, I give you my heart."

I repeat the vows, my heart soaring as we pledge the rest of our lives together. My voice cracks a little on the last line. "On this wonderful day, with our dear ones around us, I give you my heart."

Greg squeezes my hand. "I love you."

"Please stand," the celebrant says, "for the tying of the Celtic Joining Cord, a symbol from Maggie's Scottish heritage."

Holding long loops of a soft golden cord in one

hand, he crisscrosses one end around our joined ring hands and ties it. Then he gives the other end to Skylar who confidently walks among our guests, weaving the golden cord around them. When everyone is joined, she brings the free end back to the celebrant. He ties it neatly to the cord around our hands, then holds them up to the gathered crowd.

"The circle is complete. Maggie and Greg, this golden cord represents the joining of your love and the promises you have made to each other in the presence of these witnesses. The cord is strong, and will hold you through the challenges of the future. It ties you now as partners for life."

He lowers our hands and turns us to face our family and friends.

"Skylar has woven this cord of love from Maggie and Greg to everyone here. Wherever you are in the world, it joins you all in support of their marriage." He turns back to us. "Now, by the power invested in me by the state of California, I pronounce you husband and wife."

The crowd cheers and throws rose petals. Greg pulls me into his arms and kisses me lovingly. I feel so safe in his arms, and the years of loneliness fall away. Our family and friends surround us, the golden cord getting tangled up, pulling us even closer together. Laughter erupts as we try to pull apart.

"How is it that families always end up in a mess like this?" Jenna's words make me smile, and I pull her closer, so glad we made it through as friends.

The celebrant coils the golden cord into a Celtic box, and Skylar presents it to us with a curtsey. The strains of a fiddle fill the air with the first triumphant notes of The Earl of Errol's Reel, my absolute favorite Scottish tune, and my heart rises even higher with the music.

Hotel staff move in with trays of champagne, and the photographer corrals us all as she snaps pictures I will treasure from this magical day. It's a whirlwind of organized chaos, and I lean into it, my cheeks almost hurting from smiling so much. Greg doesn't let me go, his strong arms around my waist, his eyes always on me. I am loved, and it is truly a delight.

"Mr. and Mrs. Warren, ladies and gentlemen. Dinner is served."

A magnificent circular table stands in the center of the room with cascades of sapphire orchids that tumble down the sides. There are tall candles in glass bowls on brilliant white table linen. Shining silverware, crystal glasses and crisp, white napkins complete the atmosphere of an intimate celebration dinner.

Barb asks a blessing on the meal, the wine flows, and happy conversation fills the air. Our meal reflects our international family: wild Scottish salmon from the rivers of my ancestors and D-Bar Beef Wellington from Barb and Doug's ranch. Greg and I share tastes of the dishes in between soft kisses, with hands entwined.

After the main course, Greg stands to make his speech, and the room quiets. I've seen him take the stage at huge conferences as an accomplished speaker, but today, he can't seem to get started. He clears his throat, takes a sip of water, and then smiles at the faces looking up at him.

"Thank you all for coming, some of you from a long way away. Maggie and I are so thrilled that you are here to celebrate our new beginning. We love you all." He turns to me, dark eyes full of love. "Now I want to tell you about my beautiful Maggie. She was a good friend from work in the past, and when we met again, she brought sunlight back into my life." He pauses. "Well, as much sunlight as you can bring to an English autumn." Laughter fills the room. "Today, I'm awed and amazed that she has agreed to become my wife and my life partner."

He looks around at the gathered crowd, our family and close friends. "Maggie and I are not spring chickens. We have both suffered sadness and loss – as have you all." His eyes rest on his children. "We're not forgetting our past loves, or the lives we lived before. But we're choosing to go on together."

"When Doug and I go hunting in the Payette National Forest, we have to take a guide with us." He pauses for a moment, catching his best friend's eye. "Because we always get lost." There are great hoots of laughter at this. "And we need a guide to get us home. As we do in life. Three years ago, I lost my guide, and I've been wandering around, lost in the dark forest. I didn't think I would ever see the sun again. Then out of the blue – literally in the blue sky on a flight to Edinburgh – Maggie came into my life again."

Greg looks at me, and everyone else fades away. "I was given a second chance at happiness." He lifts my fingers to his lips and kisses them. "I love you, Maggie, and I'm so excited to begin this next phase of our life together."

He leans down, and I lift my face for his gentle kiss. Applause rings out around us. Doug raises his glass. "To Maggie and Greg!"

Everyone joins in and the toast echoes around the room. Neither of us like traditional wedding cake, so we have sticky, toffee pudding from the English Lake District, my favorite dessert, followed by European cheeses and fruit.

As we finish, the strains of Sting's Fields of Gold echo through the room, and I remember the night we drove through the dark out of London. Our first limo ride together. Greg escorts me to the dance floor. As we sway together, he whispers, "I love you, Maggie Warren." I am in heaven, and this is only the beginning.

After the song ends, we dance with our children. I relax as Harry leads me expertly around the floor, and Greg dances with Jenna, and then with Susan, as I waltz with Todd. Peace is restored and even though the inevitable storms will come – as they always will with family – I know that we will make it through.

The night speeds on, and soon, it's time to go. Greg hugs Susan and the girls then shakes hands with Todd. He holds Jenna for an extra second before letting her go, a contented smile on his face. I only hope his daughter can find the same happiness we have.

Sam and Luke hold hands as they both hug me goodbye. Sky and Shelby throw the remaining rose petals over Harry as he kisses my cheek and ducks away, laughing at them. We can leave now, knowing our family is safe and happy.

"New Zealand, here we come!" Greg says. Everyone throws more confetti and we get into the wedding limo.

As we drive away, I turn to look at Greg. I didn't believe that real love could come again for me. The sort where the world is bursting with joy because you've found a wonderful man whom you love and who loves you back.

But I'm here with him now, and Greg Warren is the special man in my life. For fun and travel, for sharing troubles and adventures.

For love, second time around.

Available now:
Love Will Find A Way

Jenna Warren is an Idaho ranch girl who loves her Appaloosa horse, Blue, and the freedom she has to live her life the way she wants to. But she's increasingly aware that she has never really seen the world, let alone experienced real love, and she hasn't found her purpose.

Daniel Martin is a British schoolteacher, bound by duty to a desperate family situation, and struggling to find his own path as a musician.

When Jenna and Dan meet at a family wedding, they are instantly attracted to each other, but Dan has to leave for Britain the next day. As Jenna follows him back to Summerfield village, a family conflict ignites, tearing their new love apart.

In this sweet romance, set between Idaho and the English countryside, in Japan and tropical Australia, can Jenna and Dan's love find a way through the obstacles that keep them apart?

More sweet romances coming soon. Sign up to be notified of the next book in the Summerfield Village sweet romance series, as well as reader giveaways:

www.PennyAppleton.com/signup

About Penny Appleton

Penny Appleton is the pen name of a mother and daughter team from the south-west of England. One of us is a *New York Times* and *USA Today* best-selling author in another genre.

We both enjoy traveling and many of the stories contain aspects of our adventures. Some of our favorite romance authors include Danielle Steele and Nora Roberts, plus we love The Thorn Birds by Colleen McCulloch, as well as Jane Austen and Stephenie Meyer.

Our favorite movies include Legends of the Fall, A Room with a View, and The Notebook. We both enjoy walking in nature, and a gin & tonic while watching the sun go down.

We are good friends … although sometimes we want to strangle each other! Family relationships are at the heart of our books.

www.PennyAppleton.com

(e) penny@pennyappleton.com
www.facebook.com/pennyappletonauthor

Acknowledgements

Thanks to my proofreaders Liz Dexter and Arnetta Jackson, and to Jane at JD Smith Design for the cover design.